5大方法，快速翻轉你的英語單字力！

Easy to Learn Vocabulary

背單字有好方法

Robert Shih /主編

Howie Philips /著

張中倩 /譯

背單字有好方法

現在是英語的時代！商業貿易、讀書考試、查資料、拓展視野、甚至上網交友，無不展現英語的重要性。不懂英語不但缺乏競爭力，而且隨時可能面臨遭受淘汰的危機。

但是即使具備基本的英語能力，也不可因此而自滿。畢竟在專業的領域上或者是重大考試中，精通英語是必備才能之一。而要提升英語聽說讀寫能力，則必定要奠定在深厚的單字實力之上。唯有掌握大量實用單字，才能辯才無礙、下筆成章、強化聽說讀寫能力！

然而現代人生活忙碌，上班族工作量大，回家只想倒頭大睡；學生熬夜唸書，書怎麼讀也讀不完，如何在最短的時間內記憶最多的單字，加強英語能力正是大家最關心的課題。

「背單字有方法」針對快速、有效的需求，統整英語中最常用的單字，分門別類，有系統列出，讓讀者快速瀏覽，迅速記憶。每個單字都搭配二組例句及會話範例，加速學習效果，各類單字流暢運用於指掌之間，是學生提升英語聽說讀寫成績的必備參考書，也是上班族於百忙中抽空進修的良師益友。讀好本書保證NEW TOEIC、 GEPT、 TOEFL、 IELTS、基測、統測、公職考試，All Pass。

編者的話

567單字學習秘法

聽各行各業傑出人物在TED 中的演講，是我每天的功課和習慣，其中令我最敬佩的，就是外語名師龍飛虎在TED 的演講中提到的：1000單，就含蓋了85% 會話必備單字。5個原則、7個動作，6個月就能學會外語了。

好東西要和好朋友分享，在這裡特別推薦給有心想學外語的讀者。

你是不是常有這樣的困擾：7000單，10000單，背了又忘，忘了又背，老是背不起來。

你其實可以不用那麼累。記住外語名師在 TED 的演講，你真的可以躺著學，輕鬆說。

567外語學習秘法即是：5 個原則、7 個行動，6 個月快速學會外語的方法。

5 個原則

1. **專注**：專注於你有興趣的那種英語內容。
2. **溝通**：把英語當作溝通工具使用。
3. **聊天**：不要從英語中猜意思，而要從交流中了解意思。
4. **大腦**：訓練你的大腦，讓它接受英語的聲調。
5. **心情**：高興、放鬆、好奇，您會很快學好英語。

7 個動作

1. **核心單字**：學英語，記1000個單字，就已含蓋了日常會話85% 的內容。
2. **大量聽**：躺著背、躺著學、躺著聽、坐著聽、開車聽、走路聽，最好。
3. **大量學**：學英語，只要會10個動詞、10個名詞和10個形容詞，再擴充和聯想，你就可以脫口說出1000句會話。
4. **專注**：學英語專注於理解意思，要優先於理解單字。
5. **模仿**：學英語，一定要模仿老外的面部表情和面部運動。
6. **英語父母**：英語父母對你，會像對待牙牙學語的嬰兒一樣， 耐心教你。
7. **左右腦圖像記憶**：連接大腦圖像記憶和聯想法，印象會較深刻，而且長久。

什麼是學外語最好、最有效的方法，相信每個人的答案和經驗都不一樣。因為每個人的學習習慣並不盡相同，吸收能力也不一樣。有些人喜歡到當地學習、有些人喜歡啃文法書、有些人喜歡嘗試新奇獨特的方法，體驗與眾不同的學習方式。不管哪一種方法，自己能吸收的效果好，就是最有效的學習方式。

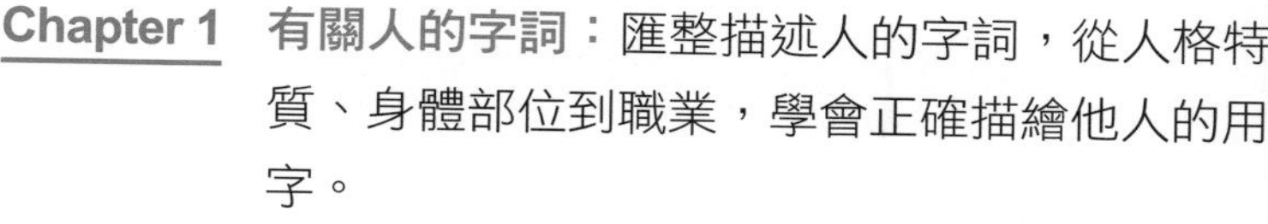

學習重點

Chapter 1 有關人的字詞：匯整描述人的字詞，從人格特質、身體部位到職業，學會正確描繪他人的用字。

Chapter 2 學校：關於學校上課的用字，也都是我們日常生活的常用字哦！

Chapter 3 家庭：本章教你關於房屋、建築物裡一些器具的說法。

Chapter 4 食物和飲料：各種飲食的英語怎麼說，餐廳點菜要怎麼點，本章為您揭曉答案。

Chapter 5 不同的地點：要去哪裡，形容東西的位置，必備單字精采呈現。

Chapter 6 常用動詞：動詞是英語句子的靈魂，熟悉使用頻率最高的動詞，必能讓您聽說讀寫暢行無阻。

Chapter 7 不可不知的名詞：絕對要知道的名詞有哪些？讀了本章讓您在考試、進修方面大有斬獲。

Chapter 8 重要的形容詞和副詞：要說出漂亮句子、寫出絕佳文章，別忘了學學形容詞和副詞，讓你的英語更加有風味喔！

【本書特色】

1. 道地英語，學習不怕出錯：為提供學習者最新最精確的英語內容，特聘專業英語老師撰寫教材，遣辭用字實用道地，讓您標準英語朗朗上口。

2. 各類實用單字，瞬間記憶：本書有系統地將單字分門別類，彙整實用度高的必備單字，讓您運用最短時間，迅速累積單字量。

3. 嚴謹編撰，專業錄音：由專業外籍錄音名師精心錄製而成的學習MP3，發音純正標準，讓您搭配本書使用，學習正確發音、自然語調，聽力同步提升。

4. 句型會話，流利運用：運用例句及會話方式呈現每個單字的用法，準確掌握單字意思，流暢應用於寫文章、對話中。

跟著本書學習，讓您輕輕鬆鬆學單字，迅速累積字彙量，省時又省力。英語聽說讀寫能力全方位發展，跟上時代潮流，掌握世界脈動，創造屬於自己的國際舞台。

【使用說明】

名師+電腦嚴選，每個單字出題頻率都達80~100%

星號數代表出題頻率，越多星星越常考

ankle 腳踝 ★★★★★

句型

» I think I twisted my **ankle** playing soccer.
我想我踢足球時扭到腳踝了。

» Jack's boots are high enough that they cover his **ankles**.
傑克的靴子長到腳踝。

句型編寫，模擬考題和貼近實用方向，每個單字的用法，準確掌握單字意思

會話

A My left **ankle** is swollen. Do you think I should see a doctor?
我左腳腳踝腫起來了。你覺得我應該去看醫生嗎？

B Try putting some ice on it first.
先用冰塊敷一下吧。

Chapter 1 有關人的字詞

artist 藝術家 ★★★★★

句型

» The young **artist** painted a lovely picture.
那個年輕的藝術家畫了一幅很美的畫。

» I think I'll study to become an **artist** at University.
我想上大學主修美術，成為藝術家。

單字活學活用

會話

A Do you know the name of any famous **artists**?
你知道任何一位著名藝術家的名字嗎？

B Yes. I think Vincent Van Gogh was very well known.
知道，我想梵谷非常有名。

會話方式精準掌握單字意思，流暢應用於寫文章、對話中

11

搭配MP3學習，效果最佳

目錄

Chapter 1

All about People

有關人的字詞

Author's Note (作者的叮嚀)

It's only fitting to start with the vocabulary that relates to us. As human beings, we first speak a language to better understand ourselves. From personality traits to body parts to professions, the following English words describe the many ways to talk about people.

要介紹字詞，當然要從和我們相關的字詞開始。人類開始說話，是為了要更瞭解自己。從人格特質、身體部位到職業，以下的字詞均用來描述人。

adult 成年人；大人 ★★★★★

句型

» When I turn eighteen, I'll become an **adult**.
一滿十八歲，我就是成年人了。

» The **adults** are in the next room playing cards.
大人們都在隔壁房間玩牌。

會話

A How come the movie ticket is so expensive?
為什麼電影票這麼貴？

B Because you're not a student anymore. You have to buy an **adult** ticket now.
因為你不再是學生了，你現在得買成人票。

ankle 腳踝 ★★★★★

句型

» I think I twisted my **ankle** playing soccer.
我想我踢足球時扭到腳踝了。

» Jack's boots are high enough that they cover his **ankles**.
傑克的靴子長到腳踝。

會話

A My left **ankle** is swollen. Do you think I should see a doctor?
我左腳腳踝腫起來了。你覺得我應該去看醫生嗎？

B Try putting some ice on it first.
先用冰塊敷一下吧。

artist 藝術家

句型

» The young **artist** painted a lovely picture.
那個年輕的藝術家畫了一幅很美的畫。

» I think I'll study to become an **artist** at University.
我想上大學主修美術，成為藝術家。

會話

A Do you know the name of any famous **artists**?
你知道任何一位著名藝術家的名字嗎？

B Yes. I think Vincent Van Gogh was very well known.
知道，我想梵谷非常有名。

aunt 伯母；嬸嬸；姑姑；阿姨；舅媽 ★★★★★

句型

» My **Aunt** Linda is my mother's oldest sister.
琳達阿姨是我媽的大姊。

» The **aunts** and uncles are coming over for supper on Saturday.
姑舅們星期六要來吃晚餐。

會話

A When will I get a chance to see **Aunty** Jill again?
我什麼時候可以再見到吉兒阿姨？

B She'll probably visit us during New Year's.
她大概新年時會來看我們。

blind 盲的；瞎的；盲目的 ★★★★★

句型

» The doctor said that if I don't wear eyeglasses, I'll go **blind**.
醫生說如果我不戴眼鏡的話，就會看不到東西。

» The **blind** man crossed the road with a walking stick.
這個盲人手持手杖過馬路。

會話

A Where are my keys?
我的鑰匙在哪裡？

B Are you **blind**? They're right in front of you!
你瞎了嗎？就在你面前啊。

blouse（婦女、兒童的）短上衣 ★★★★★

句型

» Jennifer is wearing a white **blouse** buttoned up to her neck.
珍妮佛穿著一件白上衣，扣子扣到脖子。

» Oh no! You've stained your **blouse**.
喔！不！你的上衣沾到東西了。

會話

A Is that a new **blouse** you have on?
你今天穿新上衣嗎？

B Yes, I bought it to match my new slacks.
對啊，我買來搭配我的新長褲。

bored 感到無聊的；厭倦的 ★★★★★

句型

» I' m **bored**. There is nothing interesting to do today.
我覺得好無聊，今天沒有好玩的事可以做。

» Jack was **bored** of watching golf.
傑克覺得看高爾夫球賽很無聊。

會話

A If you're **bored**, you can come over and watch television.
如果你覺得無聊，可以過來一起看電視。

B That sounds nice. There's an exciting new program I'd like to see.
聽起來不錯，有一個刺激的新節目，我滿想看的。

boring 令人無聊的；乏味的 ★★★★★

句型

» Peter never has anything funny to say. He's very **boring**.
彼得都講不出好笑的事，他是個很乏味的人。

» The concert was **boring** because I didn't know any of the songs.
演唱會很無聊，因為這些歌我都沒聽過。

會話

A What did you think of the new Arnold Schwarzeneger movie?
你覺得阿諾的新電影怎麼樣？

B I thought it was very **boring**. There wasn't enough action. 我覺得很乏味， 作場面不夠多。

businessman 商人；實業家 ★★★★★

句型

» **Businessmen** are important for the economy.
商人對經濟來說很重要。

» That **businessman** wearing the suit and tie is my father.
那個穿西裝、打領帶的生意人是我爸。

會話

A Who does Jack work for?
傑克為誰工作？

B No one. He's a self-made **businessman**.
沒有人，他是白手起家的商人。

clothes 衣服 ★★★★★

句型

» After taking a shower, Jack put on his **clothes**.
洗完澡後，傑克穿上了衣服。

» Don't dirty your **clothes**! I just washed them.
不要把你的衣服弄髒！我才剛洗過它們。

會話

A What kind of **clothes** do you like to wear?
你們喜歡穿什麼樣的衣服？

B I wear jeans and t-shirts, but my girlfriend likes to wear dresses.
我穿牛仔褲和T恤，但我女朋友喜歡穿洋裝。

confident 自信的 

句型

» Jack is **confident** that he'll do well on the English test.
傑克有自信會將英文考試考好。

» I don't feel **confident** driving a car. It makes me nervous.
我開車沒什麼自信，開車讓我感到緊張。

會話

A Why is Jennifer so shy?
珍妮佛為什麼這麼害羞？

B She doesn't feel **confident** around people.
她在人群中會感到自卑。

MP3 3

considerate (adj.) 體貼的 ★★★★★

句型

» It was very **considerate** of you to help me find a new apartment.
你真是太體貼了，幫我找到了新公寓。

» Helping elderly women cross the street is a **considerate** thing to do.
扶年老女士過馬路是件很體貼的事。

會話

A It was so kind of Jack to buy us a Christmas card.
傑克實在太好了，還買聖誕卡給我們。

B Yes, it was. He's always been a very **considerate** friend. 沒錯，他一直都是個很體貼的朋友。

consider (v.) 考慮；思考 ★★★★★

句型

» I stopped to **consider** the consequences of my actions.
我停下來思考自己的行為會帶來的後果。

» He **considered** taking a taxi to the hospital to get there faster.
他考慮搭計程車，那樣可以快點趕到醫院。

會話

A Would you **consider** working for me?
你會考慮為我工作嗎？

B Well, I like the job I have now, but I'll think about it.
我喜歡現在的工作，但我會考慮看看。

contact lens 隱形眼鏡 ★★★★★

句型

» I don't like wearing eyeglasses so I bought **contact lenses** instead.
我不喜歡戴眼鏡，所以買了隱形眼鏡。

» Ow! My **contact lens** is stuck in my eye.
噢！我的隱形眼鏡卡在眼睛裡了。

會話

A What are you looking for?
你在找什麼？

B I dropped my **contact lens** somewhere on the floor.
我的隱形眼鏡掉到地上了。

cool 涼爽的 

句型

» I can tell autumn is coming because it's getting **cool** outside.
我知道秋天快來了，因為天氣轉涼了。

» Do you want a **cool** drink before supper?
晚餐前，你想要喝杯冷飲嗎？

會話

A Is it always this hot in the city?
城裡總是這麼熱嗎？

B Not always. Sometimes a **cool** breeze blows off the river.
沒有，偶爾也會有涼風從河面吹來。

cousin 堂（表）兄弟姊妹 ★★★★★

句型

» John is my **cousin**. We've played together since we were just babies.
約翰是我表哥，我們從小一起玩到大。

» My parents have lots of brothers and sisters, so I've got plenty of **cousins**.
我父母有許多兄弟姊妹，所以我有許多堂、表兄弟姊妹。

會話

A Why don't we go hiking next weekend?
下週末一起去健行吧？

B Sorry, I can't. I have to go to my **cousin's** wedding.
抱歉，我沒空。我得去參加堂哥的婚禮。

crazy 瘋狂的 

句型

» After the accident, Uncle Bob went **crazy** and had to see a doctor.
在那次意外後，鮑伯叔叔就發瘋了，所以得去看醫生。

» That loud music is driving me **crazy**!
吵雜的音樂快把我逼瘋了！

會話

A Do you want a cigarette?
你想要來根煙嗎？

B Are you **crazy**? Those things will kill you.
你瘋了？那玩意會讓你送命的。

cruel 殘忍的 ★★★★★

句型

» It's **cruel** to tease animals.
欺負動物是很殘忍的。

» He is very kind. He doesn't have a **cruel** bone in his body.
他人很好，渾身上下找不出一點壞心眼。

會話

A Why is your brother so **cruel** to you?
你哥哥為什麼對你這麼殘酷？

B I don't know. He takes pleasure out of being mean to people.
不知道。他把快樂建築在別人的痛苦上吧。

curious 好奇的 ★★★★★

句型

» Jennifer is one of the most **curious** people I've ever met. She's always asking questions.
我認識的人中，珍妮佛是好奇心最重的人之一。她總有問不完的問題。

» I'm **curious**, have you ever worked as a journalist?
我很好奇，你是否曾經當過記者？

會話

A Sometimes it's safer not to know certain things.
有時候，有些事情還是不知道的好。

B Well, you know what they say: "**Curiosity** killed the cat."
你知道的，俗語說：好奇殺死一隻貓。

customer 顧客 ★★★☆☆

句型

» A good restaurant owner always satisfies his **customers**.
好的餐廳老闆總是能夠滿足他的顧客。

» The **customer** wanted a refund on the dress she bought.
這位顧客想要把她買的洋裝拿去退錢。

會話

A That **customer** in the computer department looks like she needs some help.
那位在電腦部門的顧客好像需要協助。

B Oh, I didn't see her. I'll go assist her right away.
喔，我沒看到她，我現在馬上過去幫忙。

deaf 聾的；聽不到的 

句型

» The doctors operated on his ears, but the old man remains **deaf** to this day.
雖然耳朵動過手術，這位老先生至今還是聽不到。

» I'm sorry, I'm a little **deaf**. Could you speak up?
抱歉，我有點耳背，你可否說大聲一點？

會話

A Why won't you have a cigarette?
何不來根煙？

B Are you **deaf**? I said I didn't want any.
你聾了嗎？我說過我不想抽。

dentist 牙醫 ★★★★★

句型

» I woke up with a toothache so I went to the **dentist**.
我今天早上起床時牙疼，所以就去看牙醫。

» Our **dentist** gives the children lollipops after he works on their teeth.
我們的牙醫在幫小孩子看過牙後，會給他們棒棒糖。

會話

A Do you know a good **dentist** in town?
你在城裡有沒有認識不錯的牙醫？

B Absolutely. My **dentist** graduated at the top of his class.
當然，我的牙醫就是班上第一名畢業的。

dumb 愚笨的 ★★★★

句型

» If you don't get a good education, everyone will think you're **dumb**.
如果你沒有受過好的教育，每個人都會以為你很笨。

» My roommate is so **dumb**! He never understands my jokes.
我室友真的很笨！他根本聽不懂我的笑話。

會話

A Let's start a pizza restaurant.
我們開家披薩店吧！

B That's a **dumb** idea! There are already several pizza restaurants in town.
那主意很蠢！城裡已經有好幾家披薩店了。

earrings 耳環

句型

» Jennifer had pretty diamond **earrings** hanging from her ears.
珍妮佛戴了很漂亮的鑽石耳環。

» I once saw a man with an **earring** through his nose.
我曾經看過一個戴鼻環的男人。

會話

A Could you help me put these **earrings** on?
你能不能幫我把耳環戴上？

B Sure. Turn around.
沒問題，轉過來吧。

engineer 工程師

句型

» Jack studied to be a civil **engineer** and now he designs bridges and buildings.
傑克主修土木工程，現在的工作是設計橋樑及建築物。

» The **engineering** students study so hard that they barely have time to relax.
工程系的學生非常用功，幾乎沒有放鬆的時間。

會話

A How do you know so much about stereos?
你怎麼會那麼懂音響呢？

B I wanted to be an electrical **engineer** when I was younger.
我年輕時，曾經想當電子工程師。

excited 興奮的 ★★★★★

句型

» I'm so **excited** to see you that I can barely stand still.
看到你，我興奮地快要站不穩了。

» The kids are **excited** about the last day of school.
孩子們在學期最後一天都很興奮。

會話

A The new phone book is here! Aren't you **excited**?
有新電話簿了！你不覺得很興奮嗎？

B Um, not exactly. Does every little thing excite you?
並沒有，這點小事就讓你感到興奮？

exciting 刺激的 ★★★★★

句型

» Jack's led a very **exciting** life. He's traveled the world and met many people.
傑克的一生過得很刺激。他到世界各地旅遊，結識許多人。

» That roller coaster ride was **exciting**. I never wanted it to end.
剛剛的雲霄飛車很刺激，我還意猶未盡呢。

會話

A What should we do tonight?
今晚要做什麼呢？

B Let's do something **exciting** like rent a sports car.
找點刺激的事吧！像是租一輛跑車。

famous 有名的 ★★★★★

句型

» Brad Pitt is a **famous** actor who has starred in many movies.
布萊德彼特是個很有名的演員，他演過很多電影。

» That restaurant is **famous** for its spaghetti.
那家餐廳以義大利麵聞名。

會話

A Do you know any **famous** singers?
你認識任何有名的歌星嗎？

B I once met Brittany Spears at an airport.
有一次我在機場遇到小甜甜布蘭妮。

female (n. / adj.) 女性；母的；女性的 ★★★★★

句型

» Including your mother, how many **females** live in the household?
你家包括你媽一共有幾位女性？

» The first dog I had was a male, but this one's a **female** and she's much well-behaved.
我養的第一隻狗是公的，但這隻是母的，她可乖多了。

會話

A Do you have any **female** coworkers?
你有任何女同事嗎？

B There's Betty in accounting. She issues our paychecks.
會計部有一個叫貝蒂的女同事，她負責我們的薪資。

fit (v.) 適合 ★★★★★

句型

» I think I'm growing. I can't seem to **fit** into my shoes anymore.
我想我還在發育，鞋子好像不合腳了。

» The suitcase is too big to **fit** into the trunk.
行李箱太大了，放不進後車廂。

會話

A Where should we sit?
我們該坐哪裡？

B I think the two of you can **fit** into the back seat of the car.
我想你們兩個可以坐在車子後座。

fit (adj.) 健康的，強健的 ★★★★★

句型

» I know I'm getting older because I'm not as **fit** as I used to be.
我知道我老了，因為我不如以前那樣強健。

» Jack eats right and exercises regularly, and so he has a **fit** figure.
傑克飲食健康，又按時運動，所以他體格健壯。

會話

A Whew! Running up those stairs made me tired.
呼！一路跑上階梯，讓我覺得好累。

B Well, you're not as **fit** as you once were.
呃 ，你已經不像以前那樣強健了。

fit (n.) 脾氣 ★★★★★

句型

» When his mother left, little Johnny had a **fit** and started crying.
當他媽媽離開時，小強尼發了一頓脾氣，然後開始哭鬧。

» Don't have a **fit**! There's more cake in the refrigerator.
別發脾氣，冰箱裡還有更多蛋糕。

會話

A What will he do if he can't go outside to play?
如果他不能到外面玩，他會怎樣？

B Oh, he'll scream and yell in a **fit** for a while before he finally settles down.
喔，他會大哭大叫，發一陣脾氣，然後才會慢慢安靜下來。

flight attendant 空服員 

句型

» On the plane, the **flight attendant** explained the safety rules.
在飛機上，空服員解釋了安全規則。

» Excuse me, **flight attendant**, when will dinner be served?
不好意思，空服員， 問什麼時候吃晚餐？

會話

A How long is the flight?
這次飛行時間多長？

B The **flight attendant** said it would take four hours.
空服員說會飛行四小時。

funny 好笑的 ★★★★★

句型

» That was a funny story. I laughed so hard I was crying.
那是個好笑的故事，我笑到流眼淚。

» Do you want to hear a funny joke?
你想不想聽個好笑的笑話？

會話

A What's so funny?
什麼事這麼好笑？

B That man's pants have fallen down.
那個男人的褲子掉了下來。

generous 慷慨的 ★★★★★

句型

» Jack made a generous contribution to charity.
傑克很慷慨的捐錢給慈善機構。

» My boss pays me well. He's a very generous man.
我的老闆付我很好的薪水，他是個很慷慨的人。

會話

A My father gave me a car for my birthday.
父親送我一部車做為生日禮物。

B Wow! That's a generous gift.
哇！這真是個慷慨的禮物。

gentleman 男士；紳士 ★★★★★

句型

» The **gentleman** in the blue suit will lead you to your seats.
穿藍西裝的男士會為你們帶位。

» If you were a **gentleman**, you'd pull out my seat for me.
如果你是位紳士，就會為我拉椅子。

會話

A Ladies and **Gentleman**! Can I have your attention please?
各位女士 ，各位先生！ 注意。

B Sit down. I think the show is about to start.
坐下來，我想表演就要開始了。

gorgeous 華麗的；美麗的 ★★★★★

句型

» That's a **gorgeous** dress you've got on. Was it expensive?
妳穿的禮服真漂亮，貴不貴？

» Jack's wife is a **gorgeous** woman with long dark hair and beautiful eyes.
傑克的妻子是個有黑色長髮及美麗雙眼的女性。

會話

A Do you think I'm ugly?
你覺得我很醜嗎？

B On the contrary, dear. You're a **gorgeous** woman.
才不呢！親愛的，妳很美麗。

greedy 貪心的 ★★★★★

句型

» Bill is a **greedy** man who only cares about money. No wonder he has few friends.
比爾是個貪心的人，他只在乎錢。難怪他沒什麼朋友。

» Don't be so **greedy**! There's plenty of food for everyone.
不要這麼貪心！食物夠讓每個人吃。

會話

A If we raised our prices we could make more money.
如果我們提高價格，就可以賺更多錢。

B You mustn't be so **greedy**. The customer's satisfaction is more important.
你不可以太貪心，客戶的滿意度更重要。

guy 男性；傢伙；朋友 ★★★★★

句型

» That **guy** in the baseball cap is my brother.
戴著棒球帽的那個人是我哥哥。

» I'm going out with the **guys** tonight to watch the baseball game.
我今晚要和朋友去看棒球賽。

會話

A Honey, why don't you come with us to watch the new Bruce Willis movie? There's going to be plenty of action.
親愛的，妳何不和我們一起去看布魯斯· 威利的新電影？應該會有很多動作場面。

B No thanks. That movie is more interesting for **guys**. I prefer romantic movies.
不，謝了。那類電影男人愛看，我比較喜歡愛情片。

hair dresser 美髮師 ★★★★★

句型

» I have an appointment with my **hair dresser** this afternoon.
我今天下午和美髮師有約。

» Jennifer's **hair dresser** gives you a free coloring when you pay for a cut.
珍妮佛的美髮師可以用剪髮價，幫你剪和染髮。

會話

A Your hair looks wonderful. Who's your **hair dresser**?
妳的髮型好棒，妳的美髮師是誰？

B His name is Peter. His shop is just around the corner from the market.
他叫彼得，他的店就在市場轉角附近。

handsome 英俊的 ★★★★

句型

» You look very **handsome** in that new suit.
你穿那件新西裝很帥。

» That's a **handsome** moustache. When did you grow it?
你的鬍子看起來很帥，什麼時候開始留的？

會話

A Joe's not that good looking, but his brother is very **handsome**.
喬不是很好看，但他哥哥非常帥。

B Joe's my husband!
喬是我老公！

healthy 健康的；舒服的 ★★★★★

句型

» It's not **healthy** to smoke and eat fatty foods.
抽煙和吃高油脂食物很不健康。

» Jack has a **healthy** appetite for pasta.
傑克對義大利通心麵有很好的胃口。

會話

A Let's go for hamburgers tonight.
今晚吃漢堡吧！

B Wouldn't you prefer a **healthy** salad?
你難道不想吃比較健康的沙拉嗎？

honest 誠實的 

句型

» She brought up an **honest** son who never lied.
她養了一個從不說謊的誠實兒子。

» I have never met an **honest** politician in my life.
我這一生中從來沒遇過誠實的政客。

會話

A Be **honest** with me. Did you like dinner?
老實告訴我，你喜不喜歡這頓晚餐？

B Well, to tell you the truth, I thought it was a bit overcooked.
嗯，老實說，我覺得晚餐有點煮太久了。

host (n. / v.) 主人；主辦；主持 ★★★★★

句型

» The **host** of the party served drinks before dinner.
宴會的主人在晚餐前先上飲料。

» Who **hosted** last year's Academy Awards?
去年的奧斯卡頒獎典禮是誰主持的？

會話

A Would you **host** our annual film festival this year?
你今年願意主持我們的年度影展嗎？

B Sure. Should I prepare a speech?
好啊，我需要準備一篇演說嗎？

housewife 家庭主婦 ★★★★★

句型

» I was a **housewife** for ten years, but now I work at a bank.
我之前當了十年的家庭主婦，不過現在我在銀行上班。

» The **housewife** made a wonderful roast dinner with boiled potatoes.
那位家庭主婦準備了一頓很棒的烤肉晚餐，跟水煮馬鈴薯。

會話

A Why are there fewer **housewives** than there used to be?
為什麼現在的家庭主婦比以前少很多？

B Because women have started working outside the home more.
因為有更多女性走出家庭，到外面工作。

humble 謙虛的 ★★★★★

句型

» Jack doesn't like to boast. He's **humble** about his achievements.
傑克不喜歡炫耀。他對自己的成就很謙虛。

» It's hard to be **humble** when you're perfect in every way.
如果你處處完美，想謙虛都很難。

會話

A I guess I've had a little success in the market these days.
我想我近來在市場上小有成就。

B Oh, don't be so **humble**! You just earned over a million dollars.
噢！別這麼謙虛！你才剛賺了一 多萬元。

humorous 幽默的；詼諧的 ★★★☆☆

句型

» The speaker told many **humorous** stories. The crowd was laughing all night.
演講者講了許多詼諧的故事，群眾整晚都笑個不停。

» Lisa told a **humorous** joke about a priest and a penguin in a bar.
麗莎講了一個關於在酒吧的神父與企鵝的幽默笑話。

會話

A Will you be the host at my wedding?
你可以當我婚禮的主持人嗎？

B Sure. Can I tell a **humorous** story about how you met your wife?
沒問題，我可以講你跟你太太認識的趣聞嗎？

interested 對……有興趣的 

句型

» Since traveling to Europe, Jack has become **interested** in different cultures.
到歐洲旅遊過後，傑克開始對不同的文化感到興趣。

» Would you be **interested** in seeing a movie tonight?
你今晚想不想看電影？

會話

A Has Jennifer always been **interested** in art?
珍妮佛一直都對藝術很感興趣嗎？

B Oh yes. Ever since she was a little girl, she has loved to paint pictures.
是的，從小時候開始，她就很喜歡畫畫。

jealous 嫉妒的；吃醋的 

句型

» I'm **jealous** of Peter's apartment. It's so much nicer than mine.
我好嫉妒彼得的公寓，比我的公寓好太多了。

» I have a **jealous** boyfriend who doesn't like when I see other men.
我有個愛吃醋的男朋友，他不喜歡我和其他男人出去。

會話

A Why should you get to go to Hawaii when I have to stay here and work?
為什麼你可以去夏威夷，而我卻必須留在這裡工作？

B Oh, you're just **jealous**. One day, you'll get to go, too.
你只是嫉妒罷了，你將來也有機會去的。

kind (adj.) 仁慈的 ★★★★★

句型

» She is a **kind** woman with a good heart.
她是個仁慈的女人。

» If everyone were as **kind** as Mother Teresa, this world would be a better place.
如果每個人都像德蕾莎修女一樣仁慈，世界會變得更美好。

會話

A I bought you some flowers.
我買了一些花給你。

B That's very **kind** of you. Thank you.
你人真好，謝謝。

kind (n.) 種類 ★★★★

句型

» What **kind** of books do you like to read?
你喜歡讀哪一類的書？

» He's the **kind** of person who would give you the shirt off his back.
他是那種會傾囊相助的人。

會話

A What's mahogany?
什麼是桃花心木？

B It's a **kind** of wood for making fine furniture.
是一種高級家具的木材。

lady 女士；淑女 ★★★★★

句型

» A **lady** always crosses her legs in public.
淑女在眾人面前的坐姿總是雙腿交叉斜放。

» Hey! That's no way to treat a **lady**.
嘿！這可不是對待淑女的方式。

會話

A Have you ever seen so many pairs of shoes?
你曾看過這麼多雙鞋嗎？

B I once knew a **lady** who had one hundred pairs of shoes.
我曾經認識一位有一百雙鞋的女士。

lawyer 律師 ★★★★★

句型

» My **lawyer** is defending a case in court today.
我的律師今天在法院辯護一件案子。

» How can I sue you if I don't have a **lawyer**?
我沒有律師，要怎麼告你呢？

會話

A That driver hit my car from behind and now I have a sore neck.
那個駕駛從後面撞上我的車，害我現在脖子痛。

B You should hire a **lawyer**.
你應該要請個律師。

lonely 寂寞的 ★★★★★

句型

» When no one else is in the house, I get **lonely**.
當家裡空無一人時，我會感到寂寞。

» As long as you have friends, you'll never be **lonely**.
只要有朋友，你就永遠不會寂寞。

會話

A What's wrong, Bill? You look sad.
比爾，怎麼了？你看起來很難過。

B Ever since my wife left, I've been **lonely**.
自從我妻子離開後，我就很寂寞。

male (n./ adj.) 男性；男性的；雄性的 ★★★★★

句型

» The **male** species is much more aggressive than the female.
雄性比雌性更具攻擊 。

» On average, **males** find jobs more quickly than females.
平均來說，男性比女性快找到工作。

會話

A I'm thinking of adopting a pet cat.
我正考慮要認養一隻貓當寵物。

B Be sure to get a **male** or else you'll end up with kittens.
最好養公的，不然最後你會有很多小貓。

manager (n.) 經理 ★★★★★

句型

» I'm the sales **manager** for this department. Can I help you?
我是這部門的業務經理，要我為你效勞嗎？

» The **manager** of the baseball club recruited a new pitcher.
棒球俱樂部的經理剛招募了一個新投手。

會話

A Who's in charge here?
這裡由誰負責？

B The **manager** is in his office. He should be able to help you.
經理在辦公室裡，他應該可以幫您忙。

married 結婚的 ★★★★★

句型

» Frank and Jill were **married** in a church in 1975.
法蘭克和吉兒1975年在 堂裡結婚。

» When I get **married**, I want to have a jazz band at the wedding.
當我結婚時，我希望婚禮上有爵士樂團演奏。

會話

A Are you **married**?
你結婚了嗎？

B Yes. I have a wife and two beautiful kids.
是的，我有妻子和兩個漂亮的小孩。

musician 音樂家 ★★★★★

句型

» Jack always wanted to become a **musician**, so he studied the violin.
傑克一直想要成為音樂家，所以他才學拉小提琴。

» At the festival, there were **musicians** from all around the world.
在節慶中，有許多來自世界各地的音樂家。

會話

A What instrument does that **musician** play?
那個音樂家演奏什麼樂器？

B The clarinet, I think.
我想是豎笛吧。

necklace 項鍊 

句型

» She wore a pearl **necklace** that matched her dress.
她戴了一條珍珠項鍊，和她的禮服很搭配。

» My grandmother gave me this **necklace** when I was ten years old.
祖母在我十歲時，給了我這條項鍊。

會話

A Somebody stole my **necklace**!
有人偷了我的項鍊！

B Oh my. We'd better call the police.
天啊！我們最好打電話報警。

neighbor 鄰居 ★★★★★

句型

» Look! Our next-door **neighbor** is having a barbecue.
看！我們隔壁的鄰居正在烤肉。

» It's after midnight and the **neighbors** still have the music on. I'm going to complain to the security guard.
已經過大半夜了，鄰居還在放音樂。我要去跟警衛抱怨這件事。

會話

A Have you met our new **neighbors** down the street?
你見過街尾的新鄰居了嗎？

B Yes. They moved here from Canada.
見過，他們是從加拿大搬來的。

nephew 姪兒；外甥 ★★★★★

句型

» My sister's son—my **nephew**—won't be able to make it to dinner this weekend.
我姐姐的兒子--我的外甥，這個週末不能過來吃晚餐。

» I had to raise my **nephew** after my brother passed away.
在我哥哥過世後，我必須照顧我的姪兒。

會話

A Is that your **nephew** in the crib?
在搖籃裡的是你的外甥嗎？

B Yes, he's a newborn. My sister just got out of the hospital last week.
對，他剛出生。我姊姊上週才剛出院。

nervous 緊張的 ★★★★★

» Jack was quite **nervous** before his final exam.
傑克在期末考前相當緊張。

» When I get **nervous**, my knees shake.
當我緊張時，我的膝蓋會發抖。

會話

A What's wrong, Lisa? You look **nervous**.
麗莎，怎麼了？妳看起來好緊張。

B I have an important job interview this afternoon.
我今天下午有個重要的面試。

niece 姪女；外甥女 ★★★★

» My sister's daughter—my **niece**—is bringing desert for dinner tonight.
我姐姐的女兒--我的外甥女，會為今晚的餐會帶甜點過來。

» I'm not really his **niece**, but I call him Uncle because he's very close to my family.
其實我不是他的姪女。我叫他叔叔，是因為他和我家往來密切。

會話

A Is your **niece** coming over to baby-sit tonight?
你的外甥女今晚會過來幫忙看小孩嗎？

B Unfortunately not. My sister believes she's still too young to baby-sit.
恐怕不會，我姊姊認為她還太年輕，不能幫忙看小孩。

nurse 護士 ★★★★★

句型

» The **nurse** assisted the doctor in the operating room.
護士在手術房內協助醫生。

» For Halloween, Jennifer wore a white **nurse's** uniform that she borrowed from her mother.
萬聖節當天，珍妮佛穿了向她媽媽借的白色護士制服。

會話

A Should I check on the patient in Room 2, doctor?
醫生，我應該去看看二號房的病人嗎？

B Please do, **Nurse** Ratchet. I think he needs some more medication.
麻 一下，羅雀小姐。我想他需要再加一些藥物。

parents 父母 ★★★★★

句型

» My **parents** both drive, but my father drives more than my mother.
我爸媽都開車，但我爸比我媽更常開車。

» When did your **parents** get married?
你父母是什麼時候結婚的？

會話

A What are you doing this weekend?
這個週末你要做什麼？

B I'm going to my **parents**' 50th wedding anniversary party.
我要去參加爸媽結婚五十週年的舞會。

partner 伙伴；拍檔 ★★★★★

句型

» My business partner bought my shares of the company.
我的合夥人買下了我在公司的股份。

» Please find a partner for the next writing exercise.
關於下一個寫作練習， 自己找一個夥伴。

會話

A Are you the sole owner of the law firm?
你是這間法律事務所的唯一老闆嗎？

B No. I have a partner in New York who manages our finances.
不是，我在紐約還有一個合夥人，他處理公司的財務。

patient (n.) 病人 ★★★★★

句型

» After the operation, the patient lay down on the bed to recover.
手術後，病人躺在床上，靜待復原。

» The doctor checked the patient's pulse, and then asked him to breathe deeply.
醫生檢查病人的脈搏，然後要病人深呼吸。

會話

A Did the patient live?
病人被救活了嗎？

B Yes, but he will stay in the hospital for a very long time.
是的，但他得要住院一段很長的時間。

patient (adj.) 有耐心的 ★★★★★

句型

» Please be **patient**. It will take me a long time to mark your tests.
請有點耐心。改你的考卷要花上一段很長的時間。

» Jack is not a **patient** man. He hates to wait for the bus.
傑克不是個有耐心的人，他討厭等公車。

會話

A I've been waiting for my order for almost half an hour.
我等我的餐點已經等了大約半個小時了。

B Just be **patient**. The waiter is quite busy, but he'll bring your food soon.
耐心點，侍者很忙，但他馬上會把你的餐點送過來。

polite 有禮貌的

句型

» A **polite** person always says "please" and "thank you".
有禮貌的人會常常說「請」和「謝謝」。

» Lawrence wasn't very **polite** to his guests. He didn't even offer them something to drink!
羅倫斯對他的客人不是很有禮貌，他甚至沒有拿飲料給他們喝。

會話

A I thought it was rude of Bill to ask so many questions.
我想比爾問這麼多問題是很無禮的。

B I know. He's not very **polite** at all.
我知道，他一點也不禮貌。

politician 政客；政治家 ★★★★★

» I want to be a **politician** so that I can change these unfair laws.
我想要當政治家，這樣我才可以修改那些不公平的法律。

» Jack thought of becoming a **politician**, but he didn't know very much about government.
傑克考慮過要當政客，但他對政府所知不多。

會話

A What's the name of the **politician** who was on the news yesterday?
昨天在新聞上看到的政客叫什麼名字？

B That's Hillary Clinton. She's the wife of Bill Clinton, the former president of the U.S.
那是希拉蕊，美國前總統柯林頓的太太。

president 總統 ★★★★★

» The first American **president** was George Washington.
美國第一任總統是喬治· 華盛頓。

» Did you know **President** Jack Chirac of France was elected for a second term?
你知道法國總統席哈克連任了嗎？

會話

A Does Britain have a prime minister or a **president**?
英國有首相，還是總統？

B A prime minister. Britain is a monarchy and only republics have **presidents**.
首相，英國是皇室制度，只有共和政體才有總統。

proud 以……為傲的 ★★★★★

句型

» Tom was **proud** of his son for passing the final exam.
湯姆以他兒子為傲，因為他通過了期末考。

» I am **proud** to be a member of the World Wildlife Federation.
我以身為「世界野生聯合會」的一員為傲。

會話

A Our son was so good in the school play.
我們的兒子在學校的話劇表演上表現得真好。

B Yes, I was very **proud** to see him on stage.
是啊，看到他在舞台上，我感到很驕傲。

relative 親戚 ★★★★★

句型

» I have many **relatives** on both sides of my parents' families.
我父母雙方都有許多親戚。

» My aunts, uncles, nieces, and nephews—all my **relatives**—will be joining us.
我的叔、伯、姨、嬸、外甥和姪子，全部的親戚都會加入我們。

會話

A Do you have any **relatives** that live outside the country?
你親戚中有沒有人住在國外？

B I have an aunt who lives in Australia and a cousin in Singapore.
我有一個阿姨住在澳洲，一個表姊在新加坡。

reporter 記者 ★★★★★

句型

» The reporter asked the politician many questions for his newspaper article.
那位記者向政客問了許多問題，是為了要寫報紙新聞。

» Laura was a reporter for the New York Times before she moved to London.
蘿拉在搬到倫敦前，是紐約時報的記者。

會話

A I don't give interviews to the Press.
我不接受媒體採訪。

B I'm not a reporter, sir. I just need your opinion for a poll.
先生，我不是記者。我只是在作民調而已。

rude 無禮的；魯莽的 ★★★★★

句型

» The waiter in that restaurant was really rude. When I said the soup was cold, he told me to leave!
那個餐廳的侍者真的很無禮，當我說湯冷掉了，他居然叫我離開。

» I don't mean to be rude, but you're talking too loud.
我不是有意冒犯，但是你實在太大聲了。

會話

A Give me that fork!
給我那支叉子！

B Don't be rude! All you have to do is say "please".
別這麼粗魯，你只需要說聲「請」，我就會拿給你了。

salesman 銷售人員 ★★★★★

句型

» The **salesman** went door to door selling soap products.
那個銷售員一家家地去賣肥皂產品。

» I once knew a **salesman** who was so good, he could sell ice to the Eskimos.
我曾經認識一位很厲害的銷售員，他厲害到可以把冰賣給愛斯基摩人（暗喻即使不需要那樣產品的人也會買）。

會話

A Who was on the phone?
誰打來的電話？

B Oh, nobody. It was just a **salesman** selling insurance.
沒什麼，只是一個賣保險的業務員而已。

scientist 科學家 ★★★★★

句型

» Galileo was a famous **scientist** who discovered that the world was round.
伽利略是有名的科學家，他發現地球是圓的。

» My brother is a **scientist**. He studied chemistry in University.
我哥哥是個科學家，他大學時主修化學。

會話

A Why is that man wearing a laboratory coat?
那個男人為什麼穿著實驗外套？

B I think he's a **scientist** in the Physics Department.
我想他是物理部門的科學家。

secretary 秘書 ★★★★★

句型

» I know a **secretary** who can type 90 words a minute.
我認識一個一分鐘可以打九十個字的秘書。

» Please ask the **secretary** to file those documents.
請吩咐秘書將那些文件歸檔。

會話

A Good morning, Thomas Parker's office. Can I help you?
早安，這裡是湯瑪斯· 帕克辦公室。有什麼可以為您效勞的嗎？

B Good morning. Am I speaking with the **secretary**?
早安， 問您是秘書嗎？

selfish 自私的 

句型

» I didn't know Tom could be so **selfish**. He won't share any of his water.
我都不知道湯姆會這麼自私，他連水都不肯分給別人喝。

» Lisa's not **selfish** at all. She's always thinking of other people.
麗莎一點都不自私，她總是為他人設想。

會話

A These are my toys!
這些是我的玩具！

B Don't be **selfish**, Billy! You can share them with your friends.
比利，別這麼自私。你可以和朋友們一起分享這些玩具。

servant 傭人 ★★★★★

句型

» Our **servants** have the week off so I'm afraid we'll have to fetch our own tea.
我們家的佣人這星期休假，所以我想我們得自己泡茶了。

» The head **servant** of the household set the dinner table.
總管把餐桌擺設好了。

會話

A May I have a cup of tea?
我可以喝杯茶嗎？

B Certainly. I'll send the **servant** to boil some water.
當然，我叫傭人去燒一些熱水。

shy 害羞的 

句型

» Jane doesn't talk much. She's quite **shy** around other people.
珍不多話，她在其他人面前相當害羞。

» Don't be **shy**, little girl! What's your name?
小女孩，別害羞。妳叫什麼名字？

會話

A Where's your daughter?
你的女兒呢？

B She's probably hiding in the bedroom. She's **shy** around other people.
她大概躲在房間裡，她在他人面前很害羞。

single 單身的 ★★★★★

» Jack's not married. He's **single**.
傑克尚未結婚，仍然單身。

» That woman must be **single** because I don't see a wedding ring on her finger.
那個女人一定是單身，因為我看到她手上沒戴結婚戒指。

會話

A Are you **single**?
你單身嗎？

B No. I have a wife and two children.
不，我有妻子和兩個小孩。

skinny 骨瘦如柴的 ★★★★★

» Jack, you must eat more. You're getting too **skinny**.
傑克，你要多吃一點，你越來越瘦了。

» She is so **skinny**, I'm afraid she'll blow away with the wind.
她這麼瘦，我怕風一來，她就會被吹走了。

會話

A Iris has lost a lot of weight, hasn't she?
愛麗絲最近瘦了許多，對不對？

B I know. She's as **skinny** as a pole.
我知道，她瘦的和桿子一樣了。

soldier 軍人；士兵 ★★★★★

句型

» My grandfather was a **soldier** in World War II.
我祖父在第二次世界大戰時是軍人。

» The **soldier** had a bullet wound in his leg.
那個士兵腿上有一個子彈的傷口。

會話

A Did any **soldiers** die in combat?
戰鬥中有任何士兵喪生嗎？

B Only two, but several civilians were injured.
只有兩個喪生，但有幾個百姓受傷了。

spoiled (adj.) 被寵壞了 ★★★★★

句型

» Tim was **spoiled** as a child. His parents bought him everything he wanted.
提姆小時候被寵壞了，他想要的東西，父母都會買給他。

» My grandparents **spoiled** me by buying me many gifts.
我的祖父母買給我許多禮物，把我給寵壞了。

會話

A Why won't you buy me the new Playstation for my birthday?
我生日時，你為什麼不買一個Playstation給我呢？

B Because you're a **spoiled** brat! This year, you're getting socks.
因為你是一個被寵壞的小孩，今年你只能拿到襪子。

spoil (v.) 毀掉；（食物）壞掉 ★★★★★

句型

» The milk will **spoil** if you leave it out of the refrigerator for too long.
牛奶若沒冷藏，太久就會壞掉。

» John **spoiled** the party by leaving early.
約翰提早離開舞會，掃了大家的興。

會話

A I have some very bad news to tell you.
我有個壞消息要告訴你。

B Can it wait? I don't want to **spoil** the beautiful sunset.
不能等一等嗎？我不想毀了這個美麗的日落。

stingy 小氣的 ★★★★★

句型

» Jack is quite **stingy** because he never spends his money.
傑克相當小氣，因為他從來不花自己的錢。

» I don't mean to be **stingy**, but you owe me one hundred dollars.
我不是故意小氣，但是你欠我一百元。

會話

A Don't be **stingy** with your chewing gum. Give me a piece.
不要這麼吝惜你的口香糖，給我一片吧！

B I only have two pieces left. Buy your own.
我只剩下兩片了，你自己去買吧。

stupid 愚笨的 ★★★★★

句型

» People will think I'm **stupid** if I don't graduate from high school.
如果我高中畢不了業，大家會認為我很笨。

» Bob is very smart, but his brother is quite **stupid**.
鮑伯非常聰明，但他弟弟卻相當笨。

會話

A Did you know Mercury is the closest planet to the sun?
你知道水星是最靠近太陽的行星嗎？

B I'm not **stupid**! I studied astronomy in school.
我又不笨，我在學校念過天文學。

successful 成功的

句型

» I hope to have a **successful** career in the future.
我希望將來能夠事業有成。

» By the suit he wears and the car he drives, I can see that he's very **successful**.
從他的西裝和座車來看，我想他是個很成功的人。

會話

A Matthew sure has a lot of money. What does he do for a living?
馬修真的很有錢，他是做什麼的？

B He's a **successful** lawyer.
他是個成功的律師。

suit (n.) 西裝 ★★★★★

句型

» He wore a striped tie with his three-piece **suit**.
他打了一條條紋領帶，來搭配他的三件式西裝。

» Do you think I look handsome in my new **suit**?
你覺得我穿新西裝很帥嗎？

會話

A What should I wear to the dinner party tonight?
我應該穿什麼參加今晚的晚宴才好？

B You'd better wear a **suit** and tie. It's a formal occasion.
你最好穿西裝、打領帶，那是個正式場合。

tongue 舌頭 ★★★★★

句型

» Please stick out your **tongue** and say "Ahh".
把你的舌頭伸出來，說「啊」。

» Jack bit his **tongue** while he was eating his steak.
傑克在吃牛排時，咬到自己的舌頭。

會話

A Did you see that? That boy stuck out his **tongue** at me!
你看到了嗎？那個男孩對我吐舌頭！

B He's only a child. Don't let it bother you.
他只是個孩子，別介意。

uncle 舅舅；叔叔；伯伯；姨丈 ★★★★★

句型

» **Uncle** Ben is my mother's brother, not my father's brother.
班舅舅，是我媽那邊的兄弟，不是我爸那邊的。

» I don't have any **uncles**, only aunts.
我沒有舅舅，只有阿姨。

會話

A Do you know where **Uncle** Ben is?
你知道班舅舅在哪裡嗎？

B He's by the table, talking to your Aunt Jill.
他就在桌子旁邊和吉兒阿姨説話。

underwear 內衣 

句型

» You're supposed to wear your **underwear** under your clothes, not over them!
你應該把內衣穿在衣服裡面，而不是衣服外面。

» My mother bought me new **underwear** and socks for my birthday.
我生日時，媽媽買了新內衣和襪子給我。

會話

A On which floor can I find the Women's **underwear** department?
女性內衣部門在哪一層樓？

B Second floor. Right next to the Men's **underwear.**
在二樓，就在男士內衣旁邊。

waist 腰 ★★★★★

句型

» His trousers are a size 32-inch **waist** and a 34-inch leg.
他的褲子是腰三十二吋，長度是三十四吋。

» Don't suck in your stomach when I measure your **waist.**
在我為你量腰圍時，不要把肚子縮進去。

會話

A She is in very good shape.
她身材很好。

B Yes, she has a slim **waist**.
是的，她的腰很細。

waitress 女侍 ★★★★★

句型

» The **waitress** served them the bowl of noodles, but she forgot to bring chopsticks.
女侍為他們上了麵，但卻忘了給他們筷子。

» Sheila applied for a job as a **waitress** at the restaurant down the street.
席拉應徵位於街尾的餐廳女侍工作。

會話

A Excuse me, **waitress**. What's the soup of the day?
女侍，不好意思。 問今日特湯是什麼？

B Today we have chicken noodle or split pea soup.
我們有雞肉湯麵或青豆湯。

wrist 手腕 ★★★★★

句型

» Bob wears a Timex watch on his left **wrist**.
鮑伯左手腕上戴了Timex的手錶。

» I think I sprained my **wrist** playing Frisbee.
我想我在玩飛盤時扭到了手腕。

會話

A Do you know what time it is?
你知道現在幾點了嗎？

B I'm afraid not. I left my **wrist** watch at home.
不知道！我把腕錶留在家裡了。

writer 作家，作者 ★★★★★

句型

» I just finished a great book, but I can't remember the **writer's** name.
我剛剛讀完一本很棒的書，但不記得作者的名字了。

» Leo Tolstoy was a Russian **writer**.
托爾斯泰是一位俄國作家。

會話

A What's the name of that American **writer** who wrote "**The Great Gatsby**"?
寫《大亨小傳》的美國作家，叫什麼名字？

B I think it was F. Scott Fitzgerald.
我想他的名字是史考特· 費茲傑羅。

Chapter 2

School

學校

Author's Note (作者的叮嚀)

The school bell rings and you sit down at your desk in the classroom. You pull out a pencil and a notebook as the teacher prepares to start the lesson. Another day, another piece of wisdom. Time to study English!

學校鐘聲響起，你會在教室的位子上坐下來。當老師要開始上課時，你會把鉛筆和筆記本拿出來。每一天都是智慧的累積。一起來學英文吧！

absent 缺席的

句型

» Jack was **absent** from school yesterday because he had a doctor's appointment.
傑克昨天缺席，因為他去看醫生。

» If you're **absent**, you should get a note from your parents.
如果你缺席的話，你要帶家長寫的字條證明。

會話

A Has anyone seen Lisa today?
今天有沒有人看到麗莎？

B She's **absent** because she's ill in the hospital.
她缺席，因為她生病住院了。

add 加上 ★★★★★

句型

» If you **add** 5 and 3, you get 8.
五加三等於八。

» Textbooks are **added** to the final price of the English course.
英文課的總費用已包括了教材費。

會話

A I can't **add** all these numbers in my head.
我沒辦法用心算把這些數字加起來。

B Do you want to borrow my calculator?
要我借你計算機嗎？

art 藝術；美術 

句型

» We painted landscapes in **art** class last week.
我們上週美術課時畫了風景圖。

» The **art** of Picasso is especially important.
畢卡索的藝術作品尤其重要。

會話

A What are those paintbrushes for?
這些畫筆是用來做什麼的？

B We are required to buy them for **art** class.
美術課規定要買這些畫筆。

attention 注意力 ★★★★★

句型

» To get the students' **attention**, the teacher clapped her hands.
那位老師拍拍手，吸引學生的注意。

» Can I have your **attention** please?
麻煩注意一下好嗎？

會話

A Jack, are you paying **attention**?
傑克，你有注意在聽嗎？

B Sorry ma'am. I was distracted by the birds outside.
抱歉，外面的鳥兒讓我分心了。

baseball 棒球 

句型

» The New York Yankees are my favorite **baseball** team.
紐約洋基隊是我最喜歡的棒球球隊。

» Michael bought a bat and a new glove for his **baseball** practice.
麥可為了棒球練習，買了球棒和新手套。

會話

A Oh my! Are you still watching TV?
天啊！你還在看電視？

B Shhh! It's the 9th inning of the **baseball** game.
噓！這是棒球賽的第九局了。

basketball 籃球 ★★★★★

句型

» It's good to be tall if you want to play **basketball**.
打籃球時，身高是一項優勢。

» Michael Jordan was my favorite **basketball** player.
邁可喬丹是我最喜歡的籃球員。

會話

A Can you dribble a **basketball?**
你會運球嗎？

B Yes, but it's hard to get such a large ball into such a small basket.
會，但是要我投籃得分，就有點難了。

behave 表現聽話；行為檢點 ★★★★★

句型

» The children were **behaving** like monkeys.
孩子們表現得像猴子一樣頑皮。

» If you don't **behave**, I won't give you any presents for Christmas.
如果你不乖，我就不給你聖誕禮物。

會話

A Are you going to sit down and **behave**, or do I have to make you leave the room?
你要乖乖坐好，還是要我請你出去？

B Sorry, sir. I'll be good from now on.
先生，對不起。從現在開始我會聽話的。

college 大學；專科 ★★★★★

» After I graduate from high school, I'm thinking of attending a technical **college**.
中學畢業後，我打算要讀技術學院。

» Jack studied business for three years in **college**.
傑克在大學念了三年的商業科目。

會話

A Do you have a **college** diploma?
你有大學文憑嗎？

B Yes, I do. I studied at Boston **College** in the 1980s.
是的，我有。1980年代時，我就讀波士頓學院。

compare 比較 ★★★★★

» If you **compare** Europe to North America, you'll see that they're very different.
如果比較歐洲和北美，你會發現它們是非常不同的。

» Paula **compared** the two pictures and saw that one was brighter than the other.
寶拉比較這兩張照片，發現那一張比另一張更亮。

會話

A You act like my mother.
你的行為好像我媽一樣。

B Don't **compare** me to your family members! I'm nothing like them.
不要把我和你的家人相比，我和他們完全不一樣。

conversation 會話；談話 ★★★★★

句型

» Jack and Thomas were having a loud **conversation** about politics.
傑克和湯瑪斯那時正大聲地談論政治。

» I was talking to Bill, but our **conversation** was interrupted by a telephone call.
我當時正在和比爾說話，但我們的談話被一通電話打斷了。

會話

A Mom, can you make me something to eat?
媽，妳能不能幫我弄點吃的？

B Can it wait, Jennifer? I'm having a **conversation** with your father.
珍妮佛，能不能等一下，我正在和妳父親談話。

copy (v.) 抄寫；複製 ★★★★★

句型

» Jane was caught **copying** the answers from her partner's test.
珍在考試時抄她同伴的答案，被逮到了。

» **Copy** your address down on this piece of paper.
將你的地址抄寫在這一張紙上。

會話

A Why are Jennifer and Lisa dressed the same?
為什麼珍妮佛和麗莎打扮得一樣呢？

B Jennifer is **copying** the way Lisa dresses, to be cool.
珍妮佛模仿麗莎的穿著，想引人注目。

copy (n.) 副本

句型

» Can I make a **copy** of that document on the photocopier?
那份文件我可影印一份嗎？

» Tim made ten **copies** of his poem to pass around the class.
提姆把他的詩印了十份，在班上傳閱。

會話

A Look at how close his signature comes to mine.
你看他的簽名和我的好像！

B It's almost an exact **copy**!
幾乎一模一樣！

debate 辯論；爭論

★★★★★

句型

» The two candidates **debated** the question of education reform on national television.
兩位候選人在全國電視上辯論教改的議題。

» I joined the **debate** club in school because I like to argue.
我加入學校的演辯社，因為我喜歡與人辯論。

會話

A Did you watch the election **debate** last night?
你昨晚有沒有看選舉辯論？

B Yes. I didn't think either of the candidates won.
有，我想兩方都沒有贏。

describe 描述 ★★★★★

句型

» Can you **describe** what the burglar was wearing?
你可以描述那個小偷的穿著嗎？

» William **described** how a computer works to the rest of the class.
威廉向班上其他人描述電腦的運作方式。

會話

A How would you **describe** your mother?
你會如何描述你的母親？

B She's small, with a round face, and very kind to strangers.
她很嬌小，有一張圓圓的臉蛋，對陌生人很親切。

develop 成長；開發；詳盡闡述 ★★★★★

句型

» After a good education, you will **develop** into a fine young man.
良好的教育，會讓你成為一個優秀的年輕人。

» Jack **developed** a plan to help the students study better.
傑克開發一個幫助學生學習的計畫。

會話

A What's that you're working on?
你正在忙什麼？

B I'm **developing** a theory on nuclear physics.
我正在研發一個有關核能物理的理論。

discuss 討論；談及 ★★★★★

句型

» Lisa and Jennifer **discussed** their jobs over lunch.
麗莎和珍妮佛在午餐時談論她們的工作。

» I'd like to **discuss** your school grades with you, Jack.
傑克，我想和你談一下成績的事。

會話

A I want to talk to you about a project I'm developing.
我想和你談談我正著手的計畫。

B Sure. Let's **discuss** it over dinner tonight.
好啊，今晚晚餐的時候討論一下吧。

divide 除；劃分 ★★★★★

句型

» 8 **divided** by 2 equals 4.
八除以二等於四。

» The teacher **divided** the cake equally among the students.
老師把蛋糕平均分給學生。

A We would like to play soccer.
我們想要踢足球。

B First, you must **divide** the class into two teams.
首先，全班要先分成兩隊。

education 教育 ★★★★★

句型

» One must get a good **education** if one wants to get a good job.
想找個好工作，就必須接受良好的教育。

» Thomas received his **education** at Harvard University.
湯瑪斯在哈佛大學接受教育。

會話

A You seem to know a lot about British writers.
你似乎對英國作家瞭解很多。

B My **education** was in English literature.
我主修英國文學。

exercise 運動 ★★★★★

句型

» John **exercises** every day. First, he runs a kilometer, and then he stretches.
約翰每天運動。他都先跑一公里，然後再做伸展運 。

» The key to a long life is a healthy diet and regular **exercise**.
長壽的關鍵在於，健康的飲食和規律的運動。

會話

A You've been sitting at that computer all day. Why don't you get some **exercise**?
你整天都坐在電腦前面，為什麼不運動一下呢？

B Good idea. I think I'll take a long walk.
這主意不錯，我想我會去散個步。

explain 解釋

句型

» The teacher **explained** the difference between "fun"and "funny".
老師解釋了fun和funny這兩個字的不同。

» Please **explain** why you're late for school.
解釋為什麼你今天遲到了。

會話

A Where are your books?
你的書呢？

B Allow me to **explain**: On the way to school, a dog chased me and...
聽我解釋，在上學途中，我被狗追，所以……

fail 失敗；不及格

句型

» If you **fail** the exam, you won't graduate from school.
如果你考試不及格，就不能畢業。

» Lisa passed all her subjects, but she unfortunately **failed** physical education.
麗莎全部科目都及格了，但遺憾的是體育課卻沒過。

會話

A Did you get your report card?
你拿到成績單了嗎？

B Yes, and I didn't **fail** a single subject.
是的，我沒有一科不及格。

flute 長笛

★★★★★

句型

» My favorite musical instrument is the **flute**.
我最喜歡的樂器是長笛。

» Kelly played a beautiful song on a **flute** at an Irish wedding.
凱莉在一場愛爾蘭婚禮中，用長笛演奏了一首很美的歌。

會話

A It must be difficult to carve a **flute**.
要雕刻一支長笛一定很困難。

B Yes. With so many holes and its long, wooden shape, I would agree.
沒錯，這樣的長度加上這麼多個洞一定很難。

friendship 友誼

句型

» Jack and Thomas built their **friendship** on trust.
傑克和湯瑪斯的友誼，建立在信任上。

» I don't think **friendship** is as important as family, but it's close.
我不認為友誼和家人一樣重要，但程度很接近。

會話

A You and Jane are always having fun together.
你和珍總是一起玩樂。

B Well, we've had a close **friendship** since we were children.
我們從孩提時代開始，就建立了親密的友誼。

fun 開心；快樂；樂趣 ★★★★★

句型

» The girls had a lot of **fun** at the amusement park.
女孩們在樂園玩得很開心。

» We had a **fun** vacation. We got to see many attractions and the weather was perfect.
我們有一個很愉快的假期，看到許多好玩的事物，天氣又很好。

會話

A Did you have **fun** at the party?
你在舞會上玩得愉快嗎？

B Not really. There weren't many people and it was kind of boring.
不怎麼樣，人不是很多，有點無聊。

grade (n. / v.) 成績；評分 ★★★★★

句型

» Our teacher **graded** the tests based on grammar and spelling.
我們老師考試評分標準是看文法及拼字。

» Jack received a **grade** of 90% on his final exam.
傑克的期末考得到九十分。

會話

A Excuse me, Mrs. Witherspoon. Are you busy?
抱歉，衛德史普老師，您在忙嗎？

B Well, I'm **grading** these exams, but I have time to talk if you need to.
我正在改考卷，但如果你有事，我可以和你談談。

grade (n.) 年級 ★★★★★

句型

» Lisa passed her 5th year of school and moved on to grade 6.
麗莎念完了五年級，升上六年級。

» After grade 12, most of the students graduated and applied for university.
念完高三後，大多數學生畢業，並申請上大學。

會話

A What grade are you in?
你現在幾年級？

B I'm in grade 7. It's much harder than grade 6.
我現在七年級了，課業比六年級難多了。

guitar 吉他 ★★★☆☆

句型

» Jack plays a six-string guitar in a rock and roll band.
傑克在搖滾樂團中演奏六弦吉他。

» The Spanish guitar is one of my favorite classical instruments.
西班牙吉他是我最喜歡的古典樂器之一。

會話

A Who's making all that noise?
誰在製造噪音？

B The neighbor downstairs plays the electric guitar.
樓下鄰居在彈電吉他。

gymnasium 體育館 ★★★★★

句型

» They're playing volleyball in the **gymnasium**.
他們在體育館裡打排球。

» The school's **gymnasium** is very large, with a basketball net at either end.
學校的體育館很大，兩端各有一個籃球架。

會話

A Where should we hang these banners?
我們要把這些旗幟掛在哪裡？

B I think they're too large for the classroom. You'll have to put them in the **gymnasium**.
我想它們太大了，教室掛不下，你得把它們放在體育館裡才行。

hand in 繳交（作業） 

句型

» Please **hand in** your tests to the teacher after you've finished.
寫完考卷後，請交給老師。

» Lisa **handed in** her English assignment late.
麗莎的英文作業遲交了。

會話

A What should we do with our math exercises?
數學習作要怎麼處理？

B Please **hand** them **in** after class.
在下課後交給老師。

improve 進步；加強；提升 ★★★★★

句型

» You'll have to **improve** your grades if you want to go to university.
如果你想上大學，成績就要再進步。

» IBM **improved** their computers by adding more memory.
IBM藉由增加記憶體，來提升他們的電腦。

會話

A Your grades are twice as good as they used to be.
你的成績比以前好上兩倍。

B Thank you. I **improved** by studying harder.
謝謝，我更用功才有進步的。

instrument 樂器 ★★★★★

句型

» My favorite musical **instrument** is the saxophone.
我最喜歡的樂器是薩克斯風。

» The band tuned their **instruments** before the concert.
樂團在演唱會前會調整樂器。

會話

A What **instrument** do you play?
你玩樂器嗎？

B I play two actually: The piano and the clarinet.
事實上，我會兩種樂器：鋼琴和豎笛。

Internet 網際網路 ★★★★★

句型

» Lisa checked her email on the **Internet**.
麗莎上網查閱電子郵件。

» The **Internet** café down the street has new computers.
街尾的那家網咖有新電腦。

會話

A I need to find some information on Australian history.
我需要找尋一些關於澳洲歷史的資料。

B Why don't you research it on the **Internet**?
為什麼不上網搜尋呢？

interrupt 打斷；中斷 ★★★★★

句型

» Lisa and Jack were talking about movies when they were **interrupted** by the telephone.
麗莎和傑克正在談論電影時，被一通電話打斷了。

» Please don't **interrupt** me when I'm talking!
我在講話時，請不要打斷我！

會話

A So, then Paula told me how upset she was over...
所以，寶拉告訴我她好沮喪，因為……

B I'm sorry to **interrupt**, but I have to go. My mother is waiting outside.
很抱歉打斷你，但我真的得走了，我媽在外面等我。

kindergarten 幼稚園 ★★★★★

句型

» Before Thomas went to grade school, he attended **kindergarten**.
在湯瑪斯上小學前，他上過幼稚園。

» I enjoyed **kindergarten** as a child because we got to color in coloring books.
我小時候很喜歡幼稚園，因為我們可以塗著色本。

會話

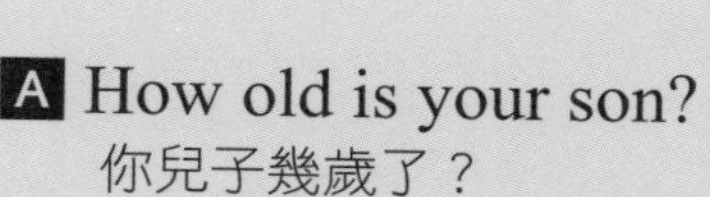

A How old is your son?
你兒子幾歲了？

B He's almost 4. He's going to start **kindergarten** this year.
快四歲了，他今年要上幼稚園了。

lesson 課 ★★★★★

句型

» The teacher prepared a **lesson** on Australian history for the class.
老師為同學準備了有關澳洲歷史的課程。

» Laura has piano **lessons** every Wednesday and Friday.
蘿拉每週三和週五都有鋼琴課。

會話

A What languages do you study?
你學了幾種語言？

B I can speak English and French, but I would like to take Spanish **lessons** some day.
我會說英文和法文，但我以後想修西班牙文。

math 數學 ★★★★★

» We learned all about addition and subtraction in **math** class today.
我們今天的數學課學了所有加減運算。

» Tim thinks the best part about **math** is trigonometry.
提姆覺得數學最有趣的是三角函數。

會話

A Are you doing your homework?
你在做功課嗎？

B Yes. We have 10 **math** questions to complete by tomorrow.
是的，我們明天要交十題數學題。

multiply 乘 ★★★★★

» 10 **multiplied** by 5 equals 50.
十乘五是五十。

» If you **multiply** any number by 0, the result is always 0.
任何數字和零相乘，結果都是零。

會話

A Tom, would you please **multiply** 7 and 9?
湯姆，七乘九是多少？

B The answer is 63.
答案是六十三。

music 音樂 ★★★★★

句型

» Lisa plays the trombone in her **music** class.
麗莎在音樂課上學習吹長號。

» We could hear classical **music** in the streets.
我們在街上可以聽到古典音樂。

會話

A What kind of **music** do you listen to?
你喜歡聽哪種音樂？

B I like all kinds, but my favorite is jazz.
都喜歡，但最喜歡爵士樂。

obey 遵守；遵照 ★★★★★

句型

» When Jack told his dog to "sit", the dog **obeyed** and sat down on the floor next to him.
傑克叫他的狗坐下。狗兒遵照命令，坐在傑克旁邊的地上。

» I always **obey** my parents because they know what's best for me.
我總是聽從父母的話，因為他們知道什麼對我最好。

會話

A Mr. Walters was caught speeding by the police again.
瓦特斯先生又因為超速，被警察逮到。

B That man never **obeys** the laws.
那個男人從來都不遵守法律。

opinion 意見；看法 ★★★★★

句型

» In my **opinion**, people shouldn't be allowed to carry guns.
我認為：擁有槍械不應合法化。

» Jill has very strong **opinions** about the rights of women.
吉兒對女權大有心得。

會話

A What's your **opinion** on health care?
你對健保有什麼看法？

B I think it should be accessible to every citizen of the country.
我覺得每一個國民都應享有這個保障。

pass 通過 

句型

» If you don't **pass** the exam, you'll fail and have to repeat grade 9.
如果你沒通過考試，就會被當掉，要重讀九年級。

» I **passed** the history exam, but just barely. I only scored 62%.
我通過了歷史考試，但只是六十二分低空飛過。

會話

A I'm nervous about my test this afternoon.
我對今天下午的考試感到很緊張。

B Don't worry, you'll **pass**. You're too smart to fail.
別擔心，你會通過的。你很聰明，沒問題的。

piano 鋼琴 ★★★★★

句型

» Even though he was almost deaf, Beethoven played the **piano** like a genius.
雖然幾乎全聾，貝多芬仍是鋼琴天才。

» Lisa played a beautiful grand **piano** with white ivory keys.
麗莎彈著有白色象牙琴鍵的美麗大鋼琴。

會話

A Do you play a musical instrument?
你會演奏樂器嗎？

B Yes, I play **piano**, but I can't buy one because they're too big to fit in my house.
會，我會彈鋼琴！但是我沒買鋼琴，因為家裡太小擺不下。

poem 詩 ★★★★★

句型

» Jack read a short, rhyming **poem** in front of the class.
傑克在全班面前朗誦了一首簡短的押韻詩。

» I once wrote a love **poem** to my first girlfriend.
我曾經寫過一首情詩給我第一任女朋友。

會話

A What's that you're reading?
你在讀什麼？

B It's a **poem** by the American poet, Robert Frost.
我在讀一首美國詩人，羅伯・佛洛斯特的詩。

principal 校長 ★★★★★

句型

» The **principal** is in charge of all the other teachers.
校長管理所有的老師。

» **Principal** Peterson called Jack into his office.
彼得森校長把傑克叫進他的辦公室。

會話

A If you misbehave, I'll send you to the **principal's** office.
如果你不乖的話，我會把你送到校長辦公室去。

B Sorry. I won't do it again.
對不起，我不會再犯了。

progress 進步 ★★★★★

句型

» Tim hasn't improved in math class at all. He's made no **progress**.
提姆的數學完全沒有改善。他沒有進步。

» Can you give me a **progress** report on the project? I'd like to know how you're doing.
你可以給我一份計畫進度表嗎？我想知道你的進展如何？

會話

A My grades are better than they used to be.
我的成績比以前好。

B Yes. I can see that you've made a lot of **progress**.
是的，我看得出來你進步很多。

project 計畫 ★★★★★

句型

» We have an art **project** due by the end of next week.
下週前，我們要交出一個美術企畫。

» Jennifer was assigned to a **project** with the other students.
珍妮佛被指定和其他學生一起做一個計畫。

會話

A What **project** are you working on now?
你現在在進行什麼計畫？

B We have to get the computers online by this afternoon.
我們在下午前必須將所有電腦上線。

pronounce 發音 ★★★★★

句型

» Tim's last name is hard to **pronounce** because it has so many consonants.
提姆的姓很難發音，因為子音太多。

» Can you tell me how to **pronounce** this word?
你可以告訴我這個字怎麼發音嗎？

會話

A He spells his name D-E-C-O-T-E-A-U.
他名字的拼法是D-E-C-O-T-E-A-U。

B Oh my! How do you **pronounce** that?
天啊！這個字要怎麼念？

prose 散文 ★★★★★

句型

» Jack composed a short piece of **prose** for his writing class.
傑克為寫作課寫了一篇散文。

» I'm not much of a poetry reader, but I really like **prose** fiction.
我不常讀詩，但卻很喜歡散文小說。

會話

A That poem doesn't have any meter or verse.
那首詩沒有任何韻律或詩節。

B It's not a poem, it's **prose**.
那不是詩，是散文。

quiz 小考 ★★★★★

句型

» There will be a short **quiz** tomorrow on the lesson you learned today.
今天上課的內容明天會考小考。

» We write **quizzes** every week and I usually score quite high.
我們每週都有小考，而我通常都考得很好。

會話

A Make sure you study your grammar tonight.
你今晚一定要記得讀文法。

B Why? Will there be a **quiz** tomorrow?
為什麼？明天有小考嗎？

review 複習 ★★★★★

句型

» At the beginning of class, the teacher **reviewed** the lesson from the day before.
每堂課開始時，老師都會複習前一天的上課內容。

» Norman **reviewed** his notes before taking the exam.
諾門在考試前會複習他的筆記。

會話

A Can we **review** the English tenses? I'm afraid I'll forget them.
我們可不可以複習一下英文時態？我怕我會忘記。

B Sure. Let's go through them one more time.
好啊，我們再複習一次吧。

science 自然科學 ★★★★★

句型

» Three common branches of **science** are chemistry, biology, and physics.
自然科學三個常見的分支是：化學、生物及物理。

» Linda's **science** teacher wore a long white laboratory coat.
琳達的自然老師穿了一件長長的白色實驗外套。

會話

A Are those equations you're memorizing?
你在背這些方程式嗎？

B Yes. I have a **science** test tomorrow.
是的，我明天要考自然科學。

semester 學期 ★★★★★

句型

» Our school year is made up of two equal **semesters**.
我們學校學制分為兩個學期。

» After the second **semester**, Linda wrote her final exams.
第二學期後，琳達考了期末考。

會話

A Are you taking psychology this **semester**?
你這學期有修心理學嗎？

B No, not until the second **semester**.
沒有，要到第二學期才會修。

silence 寂靜無聲；安靜 ★★★★★

句型

» The auditorium was filled with **silence**. Not a sound could be heard.
大禮堂裡寂靜無聲，一點聲音都聽不到。

» The priest asked for complete **silence** before the funeral service began.
在葬禮儀式開始前，神父要求大家完全安靜。

會話

A Could you turn off the TV? I need **silence** to study for my exams.
你可不可以把電視關掉？我需要安靜，才能準備考試。

B Sorry Anne. I'll make sure not to make any more noise.
安，很抱歉，我不會再製造任何噪音。

skill 技巧 ★★★★★

句型

» Typing is a good **skill** to have if you want to be a secretary.
如果你想要當秘書的話，打字是一個必備的優勢。

» It takes a lot of **skill** to be a professional sportsman.
要當職業運動員，要具備許多技巧。

會話

A What **skills** do you have for this job?
你有什麼技巧可以用在這個工作上？

B Well, I'm very good with computers and I communicate well with others.
呃，我非常擅長電腦，而且與人溝通良好。

solve 解決 ★★★★★

句型

» Mary wasn't able to **solve** the problem, so the teacher told her the answer.
瑪麗解不出這道題目，所以老師把答案告訴她。

» How should we try to **solve** the problem of world hunger?
我們要如何解決世界飢荒的問題？

會話

A I can't seem to **solve** this math problem.
我似乎解不出這個數學題。

B Maybe if you take a break, the solution will come to you later.
如果你休息一下，也許就會想出答案。

sports 運動項目 ★★★★★

句型

» The most played **sport** in the world is soccer.
世界上最多人玩的運動是足球。

» Paul is not very good at **sports**, but he likes to read.
保羅不擅長運動，但他喜歡閱讀。

會話

A What **sports** do you play?
你都做些什麼運動？

B I like baseball, soccer, ice hockey, and tennis. How about you?
我喜歡棒球、足球、冰上曲棍球和網球。你呢？

subject 科目；主題 ★★★★★

句型

» Lisa's least favorite **subject** is math. She hates math.
麗莎最不喜歡的科目是數學，她討厭數學。

» The **subject** of the author's latest book was the planet Mars.
這位作者的新書，主題是火星。

會話

A Mrs. Clyde is my **favorite** teacher.
克萊德老師是我最喜歡的老師。

B Really? What **subjects** does she teach?
真的嗎？她教什麼科目？

subtract 減

★★★★★

句型

» If you **subtract** 2 from 10, you get 8.
十減二等於八。

» For the exercises, we had to add and **subtract** a series of numbers.
我們必須做一系列數字加減的習題。

會話

A You owe me 10 dollars.
你欠我十元。

B But if you **subtract** the hamburger I just bought you, I only owe you 5.
如果你減掉我剛幫你買的漢堡，我只欠你五元。

succeed 成功

句型

» William **succeeded** at winning the math competition.
威廉贏了數學競賽。

» If you **succeed** in life, a happier life it will be.
若你的人生成功，生命會比較快樂。

會話

A Did you **succeed** at convincing Larry to come to the party tonight?
你成功説服賴利，來參加今晚的舞會嗎？

B Unfortunately not. He wouldn't listen to me.
抱歉，他就是不聽我的。

talent 才能；天份 ★★★★

句型

» Juggling is a **talent** that takes a lot of time to learn.
雜耍戲法是一項需要長時間學習的才能。

» Jack is a **talented** writer. He's very good at forming plots.
傑克是個有天份的作家，擅長編寫劇情。

會話

A This roast tastes terrible. What happened?
這個烤肉好難吃，怎麼搞的？

B I'm afraid I don't have much of a **talent** for cooking. Should we order out?
我想我對煮菜沒什麼天份，是不是應該叫外賣呢？

topic 主題

句型

» The **topic** of tonight's speech will be: "The War on Drugs".
今晚演講的主題是「毒品戰爭」。

» I have to find an interesting **topic** to write my essay on.
我得要找個有趣的主題，來寫論文。

會話

A I find political **topics** very boring.
我覺得政治議題很無聊。

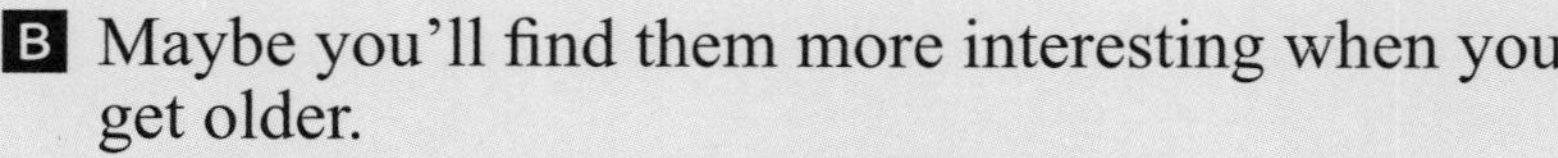

B Maybe you'll find them more interesting when you get older.
也許等你年紀大一點，就會覺得這些議題有趣多了。

trace 描繪 ★★★★★

句型

» Please **trace** the outline of this picture.
將這張照片的輪廓描出來。

» In kindergarten, Billy **traced** his hand on a piece of paper.
在幼稚園時，比利在紙上描出自己的手形來。

會話

A I have to draw a picture of a flower but I'm not a very good artist.
我必須畫一朵花，但是我不太會畫畫。

B Why don't you **trace** one from this magazine?
你何不從這本雜誌上描出一朵花來呢？

type (v.) 打字 ★★★★★

句型

» Lucy can **type** 90 words per minute.
露西一分鐘可以打九十個字。

» When I **type**, I only use two fingers.
我只用兩根手指打字。

會話

A Are you going to hand in your essay handwritten?
你的作文要交手寫稿嗎？

B No, this is only a first draft. I'll **type** it on the computer before I hand it in.
不，這只是初稿，在繳交之前，我會用電腦打出來。

type (n.) 類型；種類

句型

» What **type** of car do you drive?
你開哪一款車？

» Jack is the **type** of person who studies hard for exams.
傑克是那種會努力準備考試的人。

會話

A Which **type** of movie do you prefer: Romance or adventure?
你比較喜歡哪類型的電影：愛情片還是冒險片？

B I like adventure movies. Romance isn't my **type**.
我喜歡冒險片，愛情片不是我喜歡的類型。

underline 畫底線

句型

» Thomas **underlined** all the words he couldn't understand in the article.
湯瑪斯把文章中不懂的字都畫上底線。

» Please **underline** titles with a ruler.
用尺把標題畫起來。

會話

A How can you tell the verbs from the nouns?
你怎麼分辨動詞和名詞？

B Well, I circle the verbs and **underline** the nouns.
我把動詞圈起來，名詞畫上底線。

university 大學 ★★★★★

句型

» Harvard is one of the most well-known **universities** in the world.
哈佛是世界上最知名的大學之一。

» Jack studies English literature at Oxford **University**.
傑克在牛津大學攻讀英國文學。

會話

A What do you want to do after you graduate from high school?
你高中畢業後，想做什麼？

B I'd like to get accepted to a good **university** and study business.
我想申請進入好大學，主修商業。

violin 小提琴 ★★★★★

句型

» To play a **violin**, one must hold it under the chin.
拉小提琴時，要將琴固定在下巴處。

» Lisa performed a wonderful **violin** solo for the concert.
麗莎在演奏會時，表演了很棒的小提琴獨奏。

會話

A Do you play a musical instrument?
你會任何樂器嗎？

B Yes, I play the **violin**.
是的，我會拉小提琴。

volleyball 排球 

句型

» The white balls and the net are for the volleyball game this afternoon.

白色的球和球網，都是為今天下午的排球賽所準備的。

» Wanda served the volleyball out of bounds.

汪達將球發出了界線外。

會話

A Have you ever played beach **volleyball**?

你玩過沙灘排球嗎？

B Yes. It was great fun, but hard to hit the ball over the net in the sand.

有，那很有趣，但是在沙地上，把球打過球網很不容易。

Chapter 3

Home

家庭

Author's Note (作者的叮嚀)

In English, there is a saying: "Home is where the heart is." Whether it's in a small town, a big city, or on a farm, or whether you live in a house, an apartment, or a mansion, home is where we feel most comfortable. Knock, knock: Is anyone home?

英文有句話說：「家是心之所在。」不管你居住的地方是小鎮、大城市或農場，不論你住在房子、公寓或別墅裡，家是讓一個人感到最自在的地方。叩叩，有人在家嗎？

address 住址 ★★★★★

句型

» My **address** is 125 Anderson Road.
我的住址是安德森路125號。

» Jack wanted to mail Lisa a letter but he didn't know her **address**.
傑克想要寄一封信給麗莎，但不知道她的住址。

會話

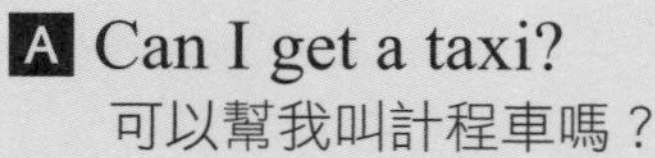

A Can I get a taxi?
可以幫我叫計程車嗎？

B Yes, sir. Would you tell me your **address** please?
好的，先生。您可以先告訴我您的住址嗎？

air conditioner 冷氣機 ★★★★★

句型

» It's so hot in here! Couldn't you turn on the **air conditioner**?
裡面好熱！你能不能開冷氣？

» We have an **air conditioner** in the car but I'm afraid it's broken.
我們的車子有冷氣，但恐怕故障了。

會話

A This restaurant is nice and cool in the summer.
這間餐廳在夏天時很舒服、很涼。

B Yes, they turn the **air conditioning** up really high.
對啊，他們把冷氣開得很強。

apartment 公寓 

句型

» Paul and his brother share a two-bedroom **apartment** in the city center.
保羅和他弟弟在市中心分租一間雙人床的公寓。

» My **apartment** is on the third floor. Should we take the elevator?
我的公寓在三樓，搭電梯好嗎？

會話

A One of these days, I'd like to buy a house.
總有一天，我要買棟房子。

B Me too. I'm getting tired of living in an **apartment**.
我也是，我厭倦了住公寓。

building (n.) 建築物 ★★★★★

句型

» His apartment is located in that red **building** by the river.
他的公寓位於河邊的那棟紅色大樓裡。

» The **building** manager has told us we aren't allowed to have pets.
大樓經理告訴我們不可以養寵物。

會話

A Can you tell me where the bank is?
你可以告訴我銀行在哪嗎？

B Sure. It's in that tall **building** across the street.
當然，就在對街那棟高樓裡。

build (v.) 建造 

句型

» They're **building** a new school on the south side of the city.
他們正在城市南邊建造一所新學校。

» Thomas used to **build** model airplanes when he was a boy.
湯瑪斯在孩提時代，曾建造過模型飛機。

會話

A What are you **building**?
你在造什麼？

B It's a miniature construction of the London Bridge.
倫敦大橋的迷你模型。

balcony 陽台 ★★★★★

句型

» From the apartment's **balcony**, you can see the entire city.
從公寓的陽台上，可以看到整個城市。

» Susan hung her laundry to dry on the **balcony**.
蘇珊把洗好的衣服掛在陽台上晾乾。

會話

A It's such a nice night out.
今晚外面天氣真好。

B Let's sit on the **balcony** and watch the sunset.
一起坐在陽台上看日落吧。

basement 地下室 ★★★★

句型

» He parks his car in the **basement** of that building.
他將車子停在那棟大樓的地下室。

» Laura had a spare room in the **basement** of her house.
蘿拉在房子的地下室，有一間客 。

會話

A Where's your cat?
你的貓呢？

B She's shy. She's probably hiding down in the **basement**.
牠很害羞，大概躲在地下室裡。

bathe 洗澡 ★★★★★

句型

» Harriet **bathes** in the evening before she goes to bed.
哈莉葉晚上洗澡後才上床。

» When I **bathe**, I use very hot water and soak for a long time.
我用很熱的水洗澡，然後泡在水裡很久。

會話

A George, please **bathe** the dog. He's filthy.
喬治，幫狗洗澡好嗎？牠好髒。

B Yes, he's been playing in the mud again.
好的，牠又在泥巴裡玩耍了。

ceiling 天花板 ★★★★★

句型

» Look up! There's a spider on the **ceiling**.
看上面！天花板上有隻蜘蛛。

» Jack had to paint the **ceiling** using a stepladder.
傑克要用摺梯才漆得到天花板。

會話

A It's too hot in here.
這裡面好熱。

B I'll turn the **ceiling** fan on to cool things down.
我會把吊扇打開，這樣會涼一點。

closet 壁櫥 ★★★★★

句型

» All of Tom's clothes were hanging in his bedroom **closet**.
湯姆所有的衣服都掛在臥室的壁櫥裡。

» If you want to clean up, there's a broom in the **closet**.
如果你想要打掃，壁櫥裡有掃把。

會話

A Where does this door lead?
這扇門通往哪裡？

B Oh, that's just the **closet**. The bathroom door is to your left.
喔，那只是壁櫥。浴室的門在你左手邊。

curtains 窗簾；布幕 ★★★★★

句型

» Lisa pulled back the living room **curtains** to let some sunlight in.
麗莎把客廳的窗簾拉開，好讓陽光照進來。

» After the play ended, the stage **curtains** closed.
戲劇表演結束後，舞台上的布幕放了下來。

會話

A What are you doing with that ladder?
你要梯子做什麼？

B I need it to hang the new **curtains**.
我掛窗簾得用到。

decorate 布置 ★★★★★

句型

» Every Christmas, we **decorate** the tree with bulbs and tinsel.
每年聖誕節，我們都會用燈泡和金屬箔裝飾來點綴聖誕樹。

» Your house looks lovely! Did you have an interior designer **decorate** it?
你的房子看起來美極了！你有請室內設計師來裝潢嗎？

會話

A What are you doing this weekend?
你週末要做什麼？

B I thought I'd **redecorate** my living room.
我想重新裝潢我的客廳。

design 設計 ★★★★★

句型

» This building was **designed** by a very famous architect.
這棟建築物是由一位非常有名的建築師所設計的。

» Paula **designed** her own wedding dress.
寶拉為自己設計婚紗。

會話

A I love your house! It's so modern looking.
我好喜歡你的房子，看起來好摩登。

B Thank you. My husband and I **designed** it ourselves.
謝謝，我老公和我一起設計的。

downstairs (adv.) 樓下

句型

» We have three bedrooms on the main floor, and a spare one **downstairs**.
我們在主樓層有三個臥室，樓下還有一間空 。

» Jack ran **downstairs** to answer the phone and almost fell and broke his neck.
傑克跑下樓去接電話，差點跌倒、摔斷脖子。

會話

A Excuse me. I'm looking for the post office. Is this the third floor?
不好意思，我在找郵局。這裡是三樓嗎？

B Yes, but the post office is **downstairs**, on the second floor.
是的，但郵局在樓下，二樓。

drawer 抽屜

句型

» Michael kept his jeans in the bottom **drawer** of his dresser.
麥可把他的牛仔褲放在衣櫃最下層的抽屜裡。

» Jane got a spoon from the silverware **drawer** in the kitchen.
珍從廚房的餐具抽屜中拿了一根湯匙。

會話

A Where do you keep your tissues?
你把衛生紙放在哪裡？

B You'll find them in the top **drawer** of that cabinet.
你可以在櫥櫃的最上層抽屜找到。

faucet 水龍頭 ★★★★★

句型

» Michael turned on the sink's **faucet** to wash the dishes.
麥可打開水槽的水龍頭來洗碗。

» The water is still running. Why don't you turn off the **faucet**?
水還在流，你為什麼不把水龍頭關起來呢？

會話

A What is that constant dripping noise?
那個滴滴答答的噪音是什麼？

B The **faucet** is leaking. We have to call a plumber in the morning.
水龍頭漏水了，我們早上要打電話叫水管工人來。

fix 修理 ★★★★★

句型

» The TV is broken. Can you help me **fix** it?
電視壞掉了，可不可以幫我修理？

» Jack **fixed** the chair so it stopped wobbling.
傑克把椅子修好了，所以它不再搖搖晃晃。

會話

A Can you help me **fix** the car?
你可以幫我修車嗎？

B Sure. I just need to get my tools from the garage.
當然，我只需要去車庫拿工具。

floor 地板 ★★★★★

句型

» The glass slipped from her hand and fell on the **floor**.
玻璃杯從她手中滑出，掉在地板上了。

» These **floors** are made of hardwood, but they're hard to clean.
這些地板是用硬木做的，不好清理。

會話

A Where is your furniture?
你的家具呢？

B I'm afraid we don't have any yet. We'll have to sit on the **floor**.
我們還沒有家具，所以得先坐在地板上。

floor 樓層 ★★★★★

句型

» John's apartment is on the second **floor** of the building.
約翰的公寓在這棟建築物的二樓。

» The elevator went up to the 15th **floor.**
電梯上到十五樓了。

會話

A Can you tell me where to find men's wear?
你可以告訴我男裝部在哪裡嗎？

B It's on the upper **floor** of the department store.
在百貨公司的上層樓面。

furniture 家具 ★★★★★

» Thomas bought his sofa at a **furniture** store.
湯瑪斯在家具店買了沙發。

» All the **furniture** in the living room was covered in plastic.
客廳中的所有家具都用塑膠套遮蓋起來了。

會話

A This room looks much bigger than it used to.
這個房間看起來比以前大多了。

B That's because all the **furniture** is missing.
那是因為所有家具都不見了。

garage車庫 ★★★★★

» Tom parked the car in the **garage** and went inside the house.
湯姆將車子停在車庫裡，然後進屋去了。

» I keep all my tools hanging on the wall in the **garage**.
我把所有工具掛在車庫的牆上。

會話

A Does the hotel have a parking **garage**?
那個旅館有車庫嗎？

B Yes. It's directly beneath us.
有，就在我們的下方。

hall 走廊 ★★★★★

句型

» Both bedrooms were connected by a long, narrow **hall**.
兩間臥室由一條長窄的走廊連接。

» Jack went into the **hall** outside his apartment.
傑克走到他公寓外的走廊上。

會話

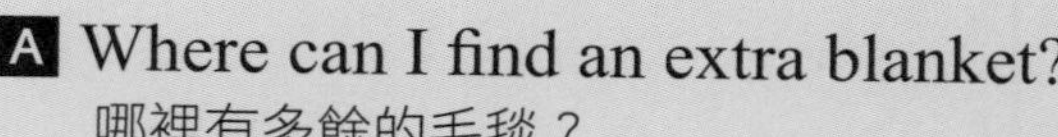

A Where can I find an extra blanket?
哪裡有多餘的毛毯？

B There's one in the **hall** closet, next to the bathroom door.
臥室門旁邊的走廊壁櫥裡有一條。

housework 家事

句型

» Jill did all the **housework** : She cleaned the dishes, vacuumed, and mopped the floors.
吉兒把家事都做完了，她洗了碗、吸地、拖地。

» We have a maid who comes in once a week to do the **housework**.
我們有一個女傭，她一週來一次，來整理家務。

會話

A Does your wife work?
你太太有工作嗎？

B Not at the moment. There's a lot of **housework** that needs to be done.
現在沒有，家裡有許多家事要忙。

lock (n.) 鎖 ★★★★★

句型

» My key won't fit in the **lock**.
我的鑰匙開不了這個鎖。

» Jack put a **lock** on his door so no one could get in.
傑克換了一個門鎖，所以沒人進得去。

會話

A Aren't you afraid someone will steal your bicycle?
你難道不怕有人會偷你的腳踏車？

B No, because I have a good **lock** for it.
不會，因為我有一個很好的鎖。

lock (v.) 鎖上 ★★★★★

句型

» Don't forget to **lock** up the store when you're finished.
事情做完後，別忘了把店門鎖上。

» Jack **locked** himself inside the bathroom by accident.
傑克不小心把自己鎖在浴室裡了。

會話

A Shouldn't you **lock** the front door?
你難道不鎖前門嗎？

B Why? I trust all my neighbors.
幹嘛要那樣做？我信任我的鄰居。

locked (adj.) 鎖上的 ★★★★★

句型

» The window was **locked** from the inside.
那扇窗是從裡面鎖上的。

» Lisa tried to open the door but it was **locked**.
麗莎試著要打開那扇門，但門鎖住了。

會話

A Is the map in the car?
地圖在車子裡嗎？

B Yes, but the doors are **locked.** Here are the keys.
是的，但車子上了鎖，這是鑰匙。

microwave 微波爐 ★★★★★

句型

» Can you heat up this soup in the **microwave**?
你能不能用微波爐把這碗湯熱一下？

» Ever since I got a **microwave**, I barely use the oven anymore.
自從我買了微波爐後，幾乎再也沒有用過烤箱了。

會話

A Should we have a snack while watching the movie?
在看電影時，要不要買一些點心吃？

B Sure. Let's pick up some **microwave** popcorn from the store.
好啊，我們去商店買一些微波爆米花吧。

mirror 鏡子 ★★★★★

句型

» Lisa looked at her reflection in the **mirror**.
麗莎看著鏡中自己的影像。

» The **mirror** is so dirty I can barely see myself in it.
鏡子髒到幾乎照不出我自己了。

會話

A I need to put on my make-up. Where's your **mirror**?
我要化個妝，你的鏡子在哪裡？

B It's in the bathroom, above the sink.
在浴室洗手台上方。

mop 拖地 ★★★★☆

句型

» After I sweep, I **mop** the floor with a bucket of hot water.
掃完地後，我用一桶熱水拖地。

» The **mop** is next to the broom in the hall closet.
拖把放在走廊壁櫥裡掃把的旁邊。

會話

A Oops! I spilled water on the floor.
啊！我不小心把水倒在地板上了。

B There's a **mop** in the corner if you want to clean it up.
假如你要清理的話，角落有支拖把。

rent (n.) 房租 ★★★★★

句型

» We can't afford to live in this part of the city. The **rent** is much too expensive.
我們住不起這區，房租太貴了。

» Cable TV and security is included in the price of the **rent**.
房租包括有線電視和保全。

會話

A It's the beginning of the month again. Do we have enough to pay the **rent**?
又是月初了，我們的錢夠付房租嗎？

B We'd better or the landlord will kick us out!
最好夠，否則房東會把我們趕出去！

rent (v.) 租用 ★★★★★

句型

» Jack and Lisa **rented** a movie from the video store.
傑克和麗莎從錄影帶店租了一部片子。

» How much does it cost to **rent** a car?
租一部車要多少錢？

會話

A Do you own this house?
這房子是你的嗎？

B Unfortunately not. We **rent** it from the neighbors.
可惜不是，我們向鄰居租的。

repair 修理 ★★★★★

句型

» The dishwasher is broken. I have to **repair** it next week.
洗碗機壞了，我下禮拜必須要修理一下。

» The TV **repair** shop is just around the corner.
電視機維修店就在街角。

會話

A This door won't shut properly.
這扇門沒辦法關合。

B I know. We have to get it **repaired**.
我知道，我們會把它修理好。

roof 屋頂 

句型

» Thomas climbed onto the **roof** of the house.
湯瑪斯爬上房子的屋頂。

» Jack looked at the stars from the **roof** of his car.
傑克從他的車頂看星星。

會話

A What's that noise above us?
上面傳來的噪音是什麼？

B I think there are squirrels on the **roof**.
我想是屋頂上的松鼠吧。

sweep 打掃 ★★★★★

句型

» Jane **sweeps** the floors clean every Saturday.
珍每週六都會把地板掃得很乾淨。

» The maid **swept** the dust under the bed.
女傭清掃了床底下的灰塵。

會話

A Why don't you **sweep** the floor?
你為什麼不掃地？

B I would, but I don't have a broom.
我想掃，只是沒有掃把。

toilet 馬桶 ★★★★★

句型

» Don't forget to flush the **toilet** when you're done.
用完馬桶之後，別忘了要沖水。

» The plumber came to fix the **toilet**.
水管工人來修過馬桶了。

會話

A Can you tell me where the men's room is, please?
問男洗手間在哪裡？

B It's around the corner, but beware: the **toilet** is broken.
在轉角處，不過要小心：馬桶壞了。

upstairs (adv.) 樓上 ★★★★★

句型

» The bathroom is **upstairs**, directly above our heads.
浴室在樓上，就在我們正上方。

» Tim was out of breath after he ran **upstairs**.
提姆在跑上樓後，幾乎喘不過氣來。

會話

A Can you tell me where to find the CDs?
可以告訴我，哪裡可以找到CD嗎？

B They're in the music department **upstairs** on the second floor.
就在樓上二樓的音樂部門。

washing machine 洗衣機 ★★★★★

句型

» Mary washes her clothes in the **washing machine**.
瑪麗用洗衣機來洗衣服。

» The **washing machine's** broken. You'll have to wash your shirt by hand.
洗衣機壞了，你得要用手洗衣服。

會話

A Is there a laundromat nearby?
這附近有洗衣店嗎？

B There's one around the corner, but the **washing machines** are expensive.
轉角有一家，但洗衣機的費用都很高。

Chapter 4

Food and Drink

食物和飲料

Author's Note (作者的叮嚀)

This chapter will probably make you hungry and thirsty. Language can never be accurate enough to describe food the way our senses of taste and smell can, but it certainly tries hard. So cook up a steak, whip up a salad, pour yourself a glass of wine, and join us at the dinner table for a feast of English words.

這一章也許會讓你感到又餓、又渴。和我們的味覺與嗅覺相比，語言永遠沒有辦法以同樣的方式，準確地描述食物，但人們還是盡量用語言來描述。所以英文裡說：煮牛排、拌沙拉、倒杯酒、到餐桌上加入我們一塊享用大餐。

alcohol 酒精

句型

» This bourbon whiskey is 40% **alcohol**.
這瓶波本威士忌含有40%的酒精。

» Kids aren't allowed to drink any kind of **alcohol**.
小孩子不准喝任何類型的酒。

會話

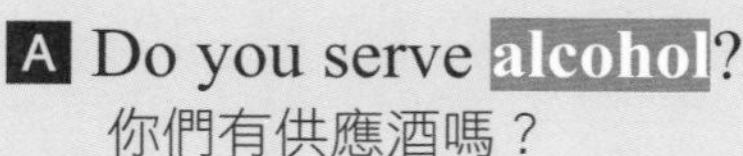

A Do you serve **alcohol**?
你們有供應酒嗎？

B I'm afraid not. Why don't you try the pub down the street?
沒有，你可以去街尾的酒吧看看！

appetizer 開胃菜 ★★★★★

句型

» Jack had a tossed salad as an **appetizer** before the main course.
傑克在主菜開始前，點了生菜沙拉當作開胃菜。

» I'm not that hungry. I think I'll only order an **appetizer**.
我沒有那麼餓，我想我只要點開胃菜就好了。

會話

A Would you like to start with an **appetizer**?
你要不要先來個開胃菜？

B Yes. Could we have a serving of escargot?
好的，先點一份蝸牛好嗎？

bake 烘烤 ★★★★★

句型

» Catherine's mother was **baking** an apple pie in the oven.
凱薩琳的媽媽在烤箱裡烤著蘋果派。

» I **baked** a fresh loaf of bread for the children.
我為孩子們烤了一條新鮮麵包。

會話

A What's that wonderful smell?
那個香味是什麼？

B Dad's **baking** chocolate chip cookies.
爸爸正在烤巧克力餅乾。

beef 牛肉 ★★★★★

句型

» This **beef** comes from Grade-A Canadian cows.
這牛肉來自A級的加拿大牛。

» The man was carving roast **beef** at the end of the buffet.
那男人正在自助餐桌尾切烤牛肉。

會話

A Would you like chicken or **beef**?
你想要雞肉還是牛肉？

B Chicken please. I'm trying to eat less red meat.
給我雞肉，我正試著少吃紅肉。

beer 啤酒 ★★★★★

句型

» Budweiser is a famous American **beer**.
「百威」是著名的美國啤酒。

» Jack ordered a bottle of German **beer** with dinner.
傑克晚餐點了一瓶德國啤酒。

會話

A What's **beer** made from?
啤酒是什麼做的？

B Hops, barley, and water.
啤酒花、大麥和水。

beverage 飲料 ★★★★★

句型

» I'm thirsty! Do you serve any **beverages**?
我渴了，你有供應飲料嗎？

» Cola is a popular **beverage** all around the world.
可樂是全世界風行的飲料。

會話

A What sorts of **beverages** do you have?
你有什麼種類的飲料？

B Well, we have water, beer, wine, coffee, fruit juice, soft drinks...
我們有水、啤酒、酒、咖啡、果汁、冷飲……

bitter 苦澀的 ★★★★★

句型

» This beer is too **bitter**! Don't you have something sweeter?
這啤酒太苦，有沒有甜一點的飲料？

» **Bitter** food leaves my mouth feeling dry.
苦的食物讓我的嘴巴覺得很乾。

會話

A Would you like a gin and tonic?
你想要喝奎寧杜松子酒嗎？

B No, thank you. Gin is much too **bitter** for me.
不，謝謝。杜松子酒對我來說太苦了。

bland 淡而無味的

句型

» This sauce is so **bland**! It doesn't have any flavor.
這調味醬太淡了！什麼味道都沒有。

» The food critic described the meal as **bland** and boring.
美食評論家把這道餐點描述為：平淡、乏味。

會話

A What did you think of the soup?
你覺得這湯如何？

B I thought it was **bland**. It needed salt or something.
我覺得太淡了，需要再加一點鹽巴或其他東西。

boil 燒煮 ★★★★★

句型

» Water **boils** at 100 degrees centigrade.
水燃燒的沸點是攝氏一百度。

» You must **boil** the water before putting in the spaghetti.
你必須要把水先煮沸，才能把義大利麵放下去。

會話

A The sauce is warming. Should I turn the heat down?
調味醬正在熱，我應該把火轉小一點嗎？

B No. Bring it to a **boil** first.
不用，先煮沸再說。

breakfast 早餐

★★★★★

句型

» I usually eat **breakfast** first thing in the morning.
我早上通常第一件事就是吃早餐。

» Thomas had a piece of toast, half a grapefruit, and a boiled egg for **breakfast**.
湯瑪斯早餐吃了一片土司、半個葡萄柚和一個水煮蛋。

會話

A Do you have ham and eggs?
你們有火腿和蛋嗎？

B Yes, but we stopped serving **breakfast** at 11:00 am.
有，但我們早餐只供應到十一點。

chopsticks 筷子

句型

» Do you prefer to eat with **chopsticks** or with a knife and fork?
你喜歡用筷子還是刀叉吃飯？

» The foreigner was having trouble eating with **chopsticks**.
外國人不擅用筷子吃飯。

會話

A Do people in India use **chopsticks**?
印度人用筷子吃飯嗎？

B No, they eat their meals with their right hand.
不，他們用右手吃飯。

corn 玉米 ★★★★★

句型

» Corn is one of my favorite vegetables.
玉米是我最喜歡的蔬菜之一。

» I love barbecued corn from the night market.
我喜歡夜市裡面賣的烤玉米。

會話

A What are these little yellow things in my soup?
湯裡面這些黃色的小東西是什麼？

B Those are kernels of corn.
那些是玉米粒。

cutlery 餐具 ★★★★☆

句型

» Please set the cutlery down in the order of fork, knife, and then spoon.
將餐具，依照叉子、刀、及湯匙的順序，擺在桌上。

» The waiter polished the cutlery until it shined.
侍者把餐具擦亮。

會話

A Excuse me, waiter. This fork is dirty.
服務生，不好意思，這叉子很髒。

B Sorry, sir. I’ll bring you a new set of cutlery right away.
很抱歉，先生，我馬上幫你拿一套新的餐具。

deep fry 炸 ★★★★★

句型

» We **deep fry** our French fries in oil.
我們的薯條是用油炸的。

» **Deep fried** food is quite unhealthy.
油炸食物相當不健康。

會話

A Is your chicken **deep fried**?
你們的雞肉是用炸的嗎？

B Normally, but we can bake it for you instead, if you'd like.
通常是的，但如果你想要的話，我們可以幫你用烤的。

dessert 甜點 ★★★★★

句型

» After the main course, Jill had ice cream for **dessert**.
在用完主菜後，吉兒的甜點是冰淇淋。

» I'd like a piece of chocolate cake for **dessert**.
我想要點巧克力蛋糕當甜點。

會話

A Would you like to see the **dessert** menu?
你想要看一下甜點菜單嗎？

B No, thanks, I'm too full to eat anymore.
不用了，謝謝，我太飽，吃不下了。

dinner 晚餐 

句型

» The Johnsons eat **dinner** every night at 6:00 pm.
強森一家人每晚六點吃晚餐。

» Thomas made **dinner** reservations at a nice restaurant.
湯瑪斯在一家很不錯的餐廳預約晚餐。

會話

A What should we eat for **dinner** tonight?
我們今晚晚餐要吃什麼？

B I don't feel like cooking. Let's order pizza.
我不想煮菜，外叫披薩吧！

entrée 主菜 

句型

» After the appetizer, the **entrée** was served.
在開胃菜後，主菜就上了。

» Jack ordered an **entrée** of roast beef, boiled potatoes, and steamed vegetables.
傑克主菜點了烤牛肉、水煮馬鈴薯及蒸青菜。

會話

A Where are the **entrées** on this menu?
菜單上主菜列在哪裡？

B Right after the appetizers and before the desserts.
在開胃菜後、甜點前。

garlic 大蒜

★★★★★

句型

» The recipe calls for lots of **garlic.**

這個食譜要用到許多大蒜。

» Jack's breath smelled of **garlic** and onions.

傑克呼出來的氣聞起來都是大蒜和洋蔥的味道。

會話

A This spaghetti is missing something.

這個義大利麵好像少了些什麼。

B Ah! We need some **garlic** bread to go with it.

啊！我們需要一些大蒜麵包搭配。

grapefruit 葡萄柚

句型

» For breakfast, Shelly ate half a **grapefruit** sprinkled with sugar.

雪莉早餐都吃半個葡萄柚，在上面灑一點糖。

» The oranges at the market were almost as big as **grapefruits**.

市場中的橘子幾乎和和葡萄柚一樣大。

會話

A Would you like something to drink?

你想喝點什麼嗎？

B Sure. Do you have any pink **grapefruit** juice?

好啊！有沒有粉紅葡萄柚汁？

hungry 飢餓的 ★★★★★

句型

» Michael's stomach grumbles when he's **hungry**.
麥可在餓的時候，肚子會叫。

» I'm so **hungry**! Don't you have anything to eat in the house?
我好餓啊！你家有沒有什麼可以吃的？

會話

A Are you **hungry**? I can make you a sandwich.
你餓了嗎？我可以幫你做一個三明治。

B No, thanks. I am thirsty, though. Do you have any juice?
不，謝了。但我渴了，你有果汁嗎？

instant noodles 泡麵 

句型

» Just add hot water to these **instant noodles**, and they'll be ready in 3 minutes.
只要將熱水加入這些泡麵中，三分鐘就可以吃了。

» Children love to eat dry **instant noodles** as snacks.
孩子們都喜歡把乾泡麵當作點心吃。

會話

A I'm hungry but I don't have time to cook.
我餓了，但是我沒時間煮飯。

B Make some **instant noodles**. They'll be ready in no time.
泡麵吧，一下子就可以吃了。

lunch 午餐 ★★★★★

句型

» The kids eat **lunch** at 12:00 pm.
孩子們十二點吃午餐。

» Laura had a soup and salad for **lunch**.
蘿拉午餐吃了沙拉和湯。

會話

A What are you doing at **lunch** time?
你午餐時間要做什麼？

B I'm going to eat and then play in the schoolyard.
我要先吃飯，然後再到操場去玩。

mango 芒果 ★★★★★

句型

» **Mangos** are in season right now so they're very inexpensive.
芒果現在盛產，所以很便宜。

» Jack had a thick glass of **mango** juice with his breakfast.
傑克早餐喝了一杯很濃的芒果汁。

會話

A Do you like green **mangos**?
你喜歡青芒果嗎？

B No, I find them too sour.
不，它們太酸。

meat 肉 ★★★★★

句型

» I love all kinds of **meat** : chicken, pork, beef, and lamb.
我喜歡各種肉：雞肉、豬肉、牛肉和羊肉。

» I'm trying to eat less red **meat**.
我試著少吃一點紅肉。

會話

A Don't you eat **meat**?
你不吃肉嗎？

B No. I'm a strict vegetarian.
不，我吃全素。

menu 菜單 ★★★★★

句型

» Mary ordered a meal from the dinner **menu**.
瑪麗從晚餐菜單中點了一份餐點。

» The appetizers are at the front of the **menu**.
開胃菜在菜單的最開始處。

會話

A Excuse me, waiter. Could we order something to eat?
侍者，抱歉。我們能不能點一些吃的？

B Sure. I'll bring you some **menus**.
好的，我會把菜單送過來。

nut 核果 ★★★★★

句型

» Almonds are my favorite kind of **nuts**.
杏仁是我最喜歡的核果。

» The squirrels gathered **nuts** and took them up the tree.
松鼠聚集核果，然後把它們拿到樹上去。

會話

A This chocolate bar has **nuts** in it!
這個巧克力棒裡面有核果。

B I'm sorry, I forgot you were allergic to **nuts**.
抱歉，我忘了你對核果過敏。

onion 洋蔥 ★★★★★

句型

» Barbara won't eat **onions** because they make her breath smell.
芭芭拉不吃洋蔥，因為那會讓她的嘴巴很臭。

» Don't you just love the smell of frying **onions**?
炸洋蔥的味道真的很棒，不是嗎？

會話

A Why are you crying?
你為什麼在流淚？

B I've been peeling and cutting **onions**.
我在剝、切洋蔥。

order (v.) 點菜 ★★★★★

句型

» I'd like to **order** something to eat off the menu please.
我想從菜單上點一些東西來吃。

» Thomas **ordered** a round of drinks for the table.
湯瑪斯為整桌的人點了飲料。

會話

A Have you **ordered** yet?
你點菜了嗎？

B No, not yet. To drink, I'd like...
還沒，關於飲料，我想要……

order (n.) 點（餐） ★★★★★

句型

» Can I get an **order** of French fries with my hamburger?
我點漢堡，可不可以順便也點一份薯條？

» Lisa placed an **order** for a large pizza.
麗莎訂了一份大披薩。

會話

A Would you like anything else with your meals?
你的餐點還需要加點什麼嗎？

B Can we get a side **order** of olives, please?
可不可以加點橄欖作為小菜？

papaya 木瓜 ★★★★★

句型

» The Thai restaurant is famous for its green **papaya** salad.
這家泰國餐廳以青木瓜沙拉著名。

» **Papaya** milk is my son's favorite drink.
木瓜牛奶是我兒子最喜歡的飲料。

會話

A What kind of tree is that?
那是什麼樹？

B By the looks of the yellow fruit, it must be a **papaya** tree.
從黃色果實的外觀看來，這棵一定是木瓜樹。

pork 豬肉 ★★★★★

句型

» Muslims don't eat **pork**. They think pigs are dirty.
回教徒不吃豬肉，他們認為豬很髒。

» Mary made **pork** chops for dinner last night.
瑪麗昨晚煮了豬排當晚餐。

會話

A Would you prefer chicken or **pork**?
你喜歡雞肉、還是豬肉？

B Chicken please. **Pork** is too fatty.
雞肉，豬肉太肥了。

Chapter 4 食物和飲料

potato 馬鈴薯 ★★★★★

句型

» Tom was served a baked **potato** with his steak.
湯姆的牛排還附了烤馬鈴薯。

» Our French fries are made from the finest **potatoes**.
我們的薯條是最好的馬鈴薯做的。

會話

A What are you going to do with that shovel?
你拿鏟子要做什麼？

B I'm going to dig up some **potatoes** from the garden.
我要把菜園裡的一些馬鈴薯挖出來。

restaurant 餐廳 

句型

» Laura reserved a table for two at her favorite **restaurant**.
蘿拉在她最喜歡的餐廳訂了兩個位置。

» I don't feel like eating at home. Let's go to a **restaurant**.
我不想在家裡吃，去餐廳吧。

會話

A Don't you serve food here?
你這裡不供應食物嗎？

B This is a bar, not a **restaurant**.
這是酒吧，不是餐廳。

salad 沙拉 ★★★★★

句型

» Michael ate a tossed **salad** before his entrée.
麥可在主菜之前，吃了一份生菜沙拉。

» There's not enough lettuce in my **salad**.
我的沙拉裡面的萵苣不夠。

會話

A I'm not very hungry this evening.
我今晚不是很餓。

B Maybe you should eat something small, like a garden **salad**.
也許你應該吃份量少一點的，像是田園沙拉。

salty (adj.) 脆的 ★★★★★

句型

» These peanuts are quite **salty**. They're making me thirsty.
這些花生蠻脆的，讓我覺得好渴。

» Eating **salty** food will give you high blood pressure.
吃鹽份過高的食物會導致高血壓。

會話

A I love sweets.
我喜歡吃甜食。

B Not me. I prefer **salty** foods like potato chips.
我可不然，我喜歡吃脆的，像是洋芋片。

salt (n.) 鹽巴 ★★★★★

句型

» Could you please pass the **salt** and pepper?
你可以把鹽巴和胡椒遞過來嗎？

» Jack's doctor told him to eat less **salt**.
傑克的醫生告訴他少吃一點鹽。

會話

A What's the difference between a lake and a sea?
湖和海哪裡不同？

B A lake consists of fresh water, and the sea is **salt** water.
湖是由淡水組成，海水是鹹水。

sandwich 三明治 

句型

» Tim made a ham **sandwich** with lettuce and tomatoes on toasted white bread.
提姆做了一個火腿三明治，在烤白土司上加了萵苣和蕃茄。

» For school, Billy's mother packed him a **sandwich** for lunch.
比利的媽媽幫他準備了三明治當學校午餐。

會話

A Do you have any lunch specials?
你們有午餐特餐嗎？

B We have a soup and **sandwich** special for $4.99.
我們有湯加上三明治的特餐，一共四塊九九。

snack (n.) 點心 ★★★★★

句型

» Paul often eats a light **snack** in between meals.
保羅常常在兩餐之間吃一點點心。

» Popcorn is a nice **snack** to have at the movies.
爆米花是看電影時的好點心。

會話

A I'm a little hungry. When is dinner?
我有一點餓。什麼時候吃晚餐？

B Not for another two hours. Would you like a **snack** to hold you over?
還有兩小時才會吃。你需不需要一點點心墊墊底？

snack (v.) 吃點心、零食 ★★★★★

句型

» At the party, the guests **snacked** on junk food.
在派對上，客人吃的點心都是垃圾食品。

» I must stop eating. I've been **snacking** all night.
我不能再吃了，我整個晚上都在吃零食。

會話

A Don't you want dinner?
你不想吃晚餐嗎？

B I'm not hungry. I was **snacking** all day at work.
我不餓，我工作時整天都在吃零食。

soft drink 冷飲 ★★★★★

句型

» Coca Cola is a popular **soft drink** around the world.
「可口可樂」是風行世界的冷飲。

» I don't like **soft drinks**. They're too sweet and fizzy.
我不喜歡冷飲，它們太甜、太多泡泡。

會話

A What kind of **soft drinks** do you have?
這裡有什麼冷飲？

B We have Cola, 7-Up, Sprite, and orange.
我們有可樂、七喜、雪碧和橘子汁。

sour 酸的 ★★★★★

句型

» These lemons are so **sour**!
這些檸檬好酸。

» This milk tastes bad. I think it has gone **sour**.
這牛奶好難喝，我想已經變酸了。

會話

A What are you going to order?
你要點什麼？

B I think I'll have the spicy and **sour** soup.
我想要點酸辣湯。

soy sauce 醬油 ★★★★★

» There's a bottle of **soy sauce** on the table, beside the hot sauce.
桌上有一罐醬油，在辣椒醬旁邊。

» Chinese dishes usually contain **soy sauce**.
中國菜中常用醬油。

會話

A Would you mind not putting so much **soy sauce** on the vegetables?
你介意不要在蔬菜上放那麼多醬油嗎？

B Of course not. I don't like my food that salty either.
當然不介意，我也不喜歡吃得太鹹。

spicy (adj.) 辛辣的 ★★★★★

» Jack doesn't eat **spicy** food because it's too hard on his stomach.
傑克不吃辛辣的食物，因為他的胃吃不消。

» If the vegetables are too bland, I can add chilies to make it a little **spicier**.
如果青菜太平淡，我可以加辣椒，讓它變得辣一點。

會話

A Do you like Thai food?
你喜歡泰國食物嗎？

B No, it's a little too **spicy** for my taste.
不，對我的口味來說，太辣了一點。

spice (n.) 香料 ★★★★★

句型

» Cinnamon is one of my favorite **spices**.
肉桂是我最喜歡的香料之一。

» Lisa loves the smells and colors of the **spice** market.
麗莎喜歡香料市場的味道和顏色。

會話

A What's your favorite thing to drink at Christmas?
你聖誕節時最喜歡喝什麼？

B I like hot, **spiced** wine because it warms the stomach.
我喜歡溫熱、加了香料的酒，因為它可以暖胃。

steak 牛排 ★★★★★

句型

» Jack likes to barbecue **steaks** in his backyard.
傑克喜歡在後院烤牛排。

» This **steak** is so tender! I barely need to use a knife.
這牛排好嫩！我幾乎不必用刀切。

會話

A What would you like to eat this evening?
你今晚想吃什麼？

B I'll have a New York **steak** with a baked potato.
我想吃紐約客牛排，加上烤馬鈴薯。

strawberry 草莓 ★★★★★

句型

» For dessert, Christine had **strawberries** and ice cream.
甜點方面，克莉斯汀點了草莓和冰淇淋。

» These **strawberries** are so red and juicy!
這些草莓都好紅潤、多汁。

會話

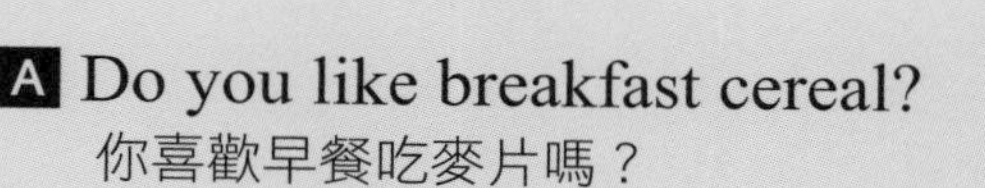

A Do you like breakfast cereal?
你喜歡早餐吃麥片嗎？

B Yes, but only with sliced **strawberries** on top.
是的，但只喜歡上面加了草莓切片的。

sweet (adj.) 甜的；（人）貼心的 

句型

» This coffee is not very **sweet**. How much sugar did you add?
這咖啡不是很甜，你加了多少糖？

» Tom likes to eat something **sweet** after dinner.
湯姆喜歡在餐後吃甜食。

會話

A I bought you a card and flowers.
我買了卡片和花給你。

B Oh, how **sweet** of you! You didn't have to do that.
喔！你真是太好了！你實在不必這麼做的。

sweets (n.) 糖果 ★★★★★

句型

» The doctor handed out **sweets** for the children.
醫生拿糖果給小孩。

» You're not allowed to eat **sweets** before bedtime.
你在睡覺前，不准吃糖果。

會話

A I have some candy if you'd like.
如果你想要，我有一些糖。

B No, thank you. I don't like **sweets** very much. They make my teeth hurt.
不，謝了。我不是很喜歡糖果，那會讓我的牙疼。

thirsty 口渴的 ★★★★★

句型

» I'm **thirsty**. Could I have a glass of water please?
我口渴，可不可以給我一杯水？

» These peanuts are making me **thirsty**.
這些花生讓我口渴。

會話

A Would you like a soft drink or some fruit juice?
你想要冷飲或果汁嗎？

B No, thanks. I'm not very **thirsty** at the moment.
不，謝了。我現在不是很渴。

tofu 豆腐 ★★★★★

句型

» Tofu is a good source of protein if you don't eat meat.
如果你不吃肉，豆腐是很好的蛋白質來源。

» Did you know that tofu is made of soy beans?
你知道豆腐是黃豆做成的嗎？

會話

A I can't eat this dish. It's got meat in it.
我不能吃這道菜，裡面有肉。

B It tastes like meat but it's actually made of tofu.
那個嚐起來像肉，但實際上是豆腐做的。

wine 酒 ★★★★★

句型

» Would you like to drink red or white wine with your meal?
你的餐點想配紅酒還是白酒？

» Jack went to a wine tasting party at his friend's house.
傑克參加在他朋友家開的品酒宴會。

會話

A Why is Tom walking like that?
湯姆走起路來怎麼那樣？

B I think he drank too much wine at dinner.
我想他晚餐時喝太多酒了。

英文勵志小語

» Heaven helps those who help themselves.
（天助自助者。）

» Heaven never helps the man who will not act.
（自己不努力，老天也沒輒。）

» When fortune smiles, embrace her.
（當命運之神向你微笑，請擁抱她。）

Chapter 5

Going Places

去不同的地點

Author's Note (作者的叮嚀)

The following English words have to do with movement and place. We all know how hard it can be to give directions. Try doing it in a foreign language! Sometimes, it can be difficult expressing movement. These words should make it much easier.

接下來的英文字都和動作、地點有關。大家都知道幫人家指引方向是很難的一件事，更不用說是要用外國語言了。有時候，描述動作也是一件難事。下面這些字應該會讓這件事變得簡單一些。

above 在……上方 

句型

» The ceiling is **above** our heads.
天花板在我們頭的上方。

» The plane was flying **above** the clouds.
飛機飛在雲的上方。

會話

A Where should I hang this picture?
我該把這張照片掛在哪裡？

B Hang it **above** the door, so everyone can see it.
掛在門的上方，這樣每個人都看得到。

airport 機場 ★★★★★

句型

» Paul took a taxi to the **airport** to catch his plane.
保羅搭計程車去機場趕搭飛機。

» Heathrow **airport** is one of the largest in the world.
希斯魯機場是世界上最大的機場之一。

會話

A What time do you have to be at the **airport**?
你幾點要到機場？

B My plane departs at 9:00 am, so I should be there by 7:00 am.
我的飛機九點起飛，所以七點前要到機場。

ambulance 救護車 ★★★★★

句型

» An **ambulance** took the patient to the hospital.
救護車將病人帶到醫院。

» Jack saw the flashing lights of an **ambulance** in his rear view mirror.
傑克從車子照後鏡看到救護車的閃燈。

會話

A I'm having chest pains.
我胸口痛。

B Should I call an **ambulance**?
需要叫救護車嗎？

area 地區 ★★★★★

句型

» This area is new to me. What is it called?
我對這個地區很陌生。這裡是哪裡？

» The prisoner escaped but he is believed to be in the area around the prison.
牢犯逃獄了，但被懷疑他仍在監獄附近地區。

會話

A Do you live in this area?
你住在這地區嗎？

B No, I live further west, on the edge of town.
不，我住在更西邊一點，在城市的邊陲。

around 在……附近 

句型

» We drove around the corner to find a parking spot.
我們開車在轉角附近找車位。

» Do you live around here? I'm looking for a good restaurant.
你住在這附近嗎？我正要找間好餐廳。

會話

A What should we do this afternoon?
我們今天下午要做什麼？

B Let's take a walk around the park.
在公園附近散步吧！

backward 向後 ★★★★★

句型

» The car started to roll **backward** down the hill.
車子開始向下坡往後移 。

» Look at that funny man walking **backward** along the street!
看看那個好笑的男人，他正在以後退的方式沿著街走。

會話

A I can't see where we're going.
我看不到我們走的方向。

B That's because the train is moving **backward**.
那是因為火車正在向後移動。

behind 在……後面 ★★★★★

句型

» Tom couldn't see the movie screen because he was sitting **behind** a tall man.
湯姆看不到電影螢幕，因為他坐在一個高個子後面。

» Watch out! There's a car coming **behind** you.
小心！你後面來了一部車。

會話

A What are you looking for?
你在找什麼？

B I dropped my keys **behind** the couch.
我把鑰匙掉在沙發後面了。

below 在……下方 ★★★★★

句型

» Don placed a ladder **below** the window.
唐把梯子放在窗戶下方。

» Boxers aren't allowed to punch **below** the belt.
拳擊手不准打對方腰帶以下的部位。

會話

A Is the paint on the top shelf?
油漆在最上面的架子嗎？

B No, it's on the shelf **below** it.
不是，在那一格的下面。

beside 在……旁邊 ★★★★★

句型

» The refrigerator stands **beside** the oven.
冰箱在烤箱旁邊。

» Jack was sitting **beside** his wife and opposite his parents.
傑克坐在他太太旁邊、他父母對面。

會話

A Where's the remote control?
遙控器在哪裡？

B Are you blind? It's right **beside** you, on the couch.
你瞎了嗎？就在你旁邊啊！在長椅上。

between 介於……之間 ★★★★★

句型

» The bank is located **between** city hall and the post office.
銀行位於市政府和郵局之間。

» Lisa sat **between** her parents: Her mother on her left and her father on her right.
麗莎坐在她父母中間，媽媽坐在她左邊，爸爸坐在她右邊。

會話

A Can you fit **between** those two cars?
這兩輛車之間的距離，你停得進去嗎？

B No, it’s too tight. I’ll have to find another parking spot.
不行，太窄了。我得再找另一個停車位。

beyond 越過；在更遠處 

句型

» Larry lives **beyond** the edge of town.
賴利住在城市的邊界外。

» No one knows for certain what lies **beyond** our solar system.
沒有人確切知道太陽系之外有什麼東西。

會話

A I can’t see the lake.
我看不到湖。

B That’s because it’s **beyond** the forest.
那是因為它在森林過去的那一邊。

bridge 橋 ★★★★★

句型

» The mayor decided to build a **bridge** over the river.
市長決定要在河上建一座橋。

» Jack crosses the **bridge** on his way to work every morning.
傑克每天早上上班路上，都會通過這座橋。

會話

A Have you ever crossed the Brooklyn **Bridge**?
你有沒有橫越過布魯克林大橋？

B No. I have never been to New York.
沒有，我從未去過紐約。

central 中央的

句型

» We live in a **central** location, right in the middle of town.
我們住在中央地區，就在市中心。

» Jack caught a train at Grand **Central** Station.
傑克在中央車站趕上了火車。

會話

A Is the hotel **centrally** located?
那個旅館位在市中心嗎？

B No. I'm afraid it's on the outskirts of the city.
不是，恐怕是位於市郊。

city 城市 ★★★★★

句型

» Mexico City is the biggest city in the world.
墨西哥市是世界上最大的城市。

» Which city do you live in?
你住在哪個城市？

會話

A I don't want to drive through the city center.
我不想要開車經過市中心。

B Then, let's take the public transportation.
那麼就搭大眾運輸工具吧。

coast (n.) 海岸

句型

» Dublin lies on the coast of the Irish Sea.
都柏林位於愛爾蘭海的海岸。

» Since Jack moved to the coast, he has a nice view of the ocean.
自從傑克搬到海岸邊後，他可以看到很漂亮的海景。

會話

A How should we get to San Francisco?
我們應該如何去舊金山？

B Let's drive along the Pacific coast.
沿著太平洋海岸開車吧。

coast (v.) 滑行 

句型

» John let off the gas and **coasted** down the hill.
約翰放開油門，然後滑行下山。

» We're going downhill. Stop pedaling your bike and **coast**.
我們正在下山途中，不用再踩踏板，只要滑行即可。

會話

A We're running out of gas.
我們的油快用完了。

B You'd better **coast** down this next hill then.
這樣的話，你最好滑行下山吧。

convenience store 便利商店 

句型

» That **convenience store** has everything you need and it's open 24 hours.
你所要的東西，那間便利商店都有，且它24小時營業。

» Would you pick me up a loaf of bread at the **convenience store**?
你可以去便利商店幫我買一條麵包嗎？

會話

A Are there any **convenience stores** open at this late hour?
這麼晚了，還有便利商店在營業的嗎？

B Sure. There's a 7-11 just around the corner.
當然，轉角就有一家7-11。

country 國家 ★★★★★

句型

» Russia is still the biggest **country** in the world.
蘇俄仍然是世界上最大的國家。

» How many African **countries** are there?
非洲有幾個國家？

會話

A What **country** do you live in?
你住在哪個國家？

B I live in Canada, but I was born in the Philippines.
我住在加拿大，但我在菲律賓出生。

country 鄉村 ★★★★★

句型

» I'm tired of the city. Let's take a drive out to the **country**.
我厭倦了城市，我們開車去鄉下走走吧。

» This **country** air is so clear and fresh.
這鄉間的空氣好乾淨，好新鮮。

會話

A Do you live in the city?
你住在城市中嗎？

B Yes, but we also have a ranch in the **country**.
是的，但是我們在鄉間有個牧場。

cross 穿越 ★★★★★

» Be careful when you **cross** the road!
過馬路時要小心。

» This path **crosses** through a national park.
這條小路穿越國家公園。

會話

A Is that a movie theater on the other side of the street?
在街的另一邊是不是電影院？

B Let's **cross** the road and find out.
過個馬路就知道了。

downtown 市中心 ★★★★★

» Michael moved **downtown**, among the skyscrapers.
麥可搬到市中心去了，住在高樓大廈中。

» If you drive **downtown**, be prepared for a lot of traffic.
如果你開車到市中心，就要做好準備，會遇上交通阻塞。

會話

A There's nothing happening around here.
這裡好無聊。

B Let's go **downtown**, where all the action is.
去市中心吧！那裡才比較熱鬧。

environment 環境 ★★★★★

句型

» If we want to continue living in this world, it's important to keep the environment clean.
如果我們想要繼續住在這世上，維持環境乾淨是很重要的。

» This environment—the area surrounding us—is a protected park.
這環繞在我們四周的環境是一個受到保護的公園。

會話

A Look at all that car exhaust in the air!
看看空氣中的汽車廢氣。

B I know. It's horrible for the environment.
我知道，這對環境有害。

farm 農場 ★★★★★

句型

» Norman keeps cows, pigs, and chickens on his farm.
諾門在他的農場上養牛、豬和雞。

» We live on a dairy farm out in the country.
我們住在鄉間的一個牛奶製品農場。

會話

A It must be nice to live on a farm.
住在農場裡一定很不錯。

B It is. There are no other houses around for miles.
是的，數哩之內都沒有其他房子。

forest 森林 ★★★★★

» This **forest** is mostly made up of pine trees.
這座森林中的樹大多是松樹。

» The farmers went hunting in the **forest**.
農夫到森林中打獵。

會話

A Have you ever heard of The Black **Forest**?
你聽過黑森林嗎？

B Yes. Isn't it somewhere in Germany?
有啊！不是在德國的某個地方嗎？

forward (adv.) 向前 ★★★★★

» Ow! You're stepping on my foot. Can you move **forward** a little?
唉呀！你踩到我的腳了，可不可以向前挪一下？

» Tom drove the car **forward** to see what was around the corner.
湯姆開車向前，去看看轉角有什麼東西。

會話

A Do you know how to dance?
你知道怎麼跳嗎？

B Sure. Take two steps **forward**, and one step back...
當然，就是往前兩步，往後一步……

hotel 旅館 ★★★★★

句型

» In New York, Lisa stayed at a 5-star **hotel**.
在紐約時，麗莎住的是五星級旅館。

» Why pay for a **hotel** when you can stay at our house?
如果可以住在我們家，你為什麼還要花錢住旅館呢？

會話

A Do you know of a good **hotel** in the area?
你知道這附近有好旅館嗎？

B There's a Holiday Inn down the street.
街尾有一家「假日旅館」。

in front of 在……前面 ★★★★★

句型

» I can't see! That tall man is standing right **in front of** me.
我看不到，那個高個子男人站在我的正前方。

» Can you read the license plate of the car **in front of** us?
你看得到我們前面那部車的車牌號碼嗎？

會話

A Where did you park the car?
你車停在哪裡？

B Directly **in front of** the supermarket.
在超市正前方。

Chapter 5 去不同的地點

inside 在……裡面 ★★★★★

» It's cold out here! Can we go **inside** the house?
外面好冷！可不可以進到屋子裡面去？

» Jack opened the door to the bank and went **inside**.
傑克打開銀行的門，然後進去了。

會話

A What's **inside** this box?
箱子裡有什麼東西？

B It's a surprise! Don't open it.
是個驚喜，不要打開。

international 國際的 ★★★★★

» The United Nations is an **international** organization.
聯合國是個國際組織。

» Howard took an **international** flight from Toronto to Bangkok.
霍華搭乘國際線班機，從多倫多飛到曼谷。

會話

A He's from Italy, she's from Brazil, they're from Russia, and I'm from the U.S.
他來自義大利，她來自巴西，他們來自蘇俄，而我來自美國。

B Oh my! What an **international** group!
天啊！這真是個國際團體。

island 島 ★★★★★

句型

» Technically, Australia is considered an island.
嚴格上來說，澳洲是一座島。

» The Hawaiian Islands are a popular tourist destination.
夏威夷群島是旅遊勝地。

會話

A What one thing would you bring to a deserted island?
如果到無人小島，只能帶一樣東西，你會帶什麼？

B Definitely some toilet paper.
絕對要帶衛生紙。

local 當地的 ★★★★★

句型

» The local people—the ones who live here—are quite friendly.
住在當地的人民相當友善。

» San Francisco's local tourist office can tell you everything about the city.
舊金山當地的旅遊局會告訴你所有有關這座城市的一切。

會話

A I would like to try some local food.
我想要嘗試一些當地食物。

B Me too. Let's go to a restaurant where the citizens usually eat.
我也是，咱們去當地居民吃飯的餐廳吧。

ocean 海洋 ★★★★☆

句型

» Whenever I swim in the **ocean**, I swallow too much salt water.
每當我在大海裡游泳時，我都會喝下太多鹹水。

» There are a lot of sharks in this **ocean**.
海洋中有許多鯊魚。

會話

A Where did the Titanic sink?
鐵達尼號在哪裡沈船？

B In the Atlantic **Ocean**, off the coast of Halifax, Canada.
在大西洋，就在加拿大海利菲斯的海岸。

outside 在……外面

句型

» It's such a nice day! Let's take a walk **outside**.
今天天氣真好，出去散散步吧。

» The man was standing just **outside** the window.
那男人就站在窗戶外面。

會話

A Where's the dog?
狗在哪裡？

B Sharon took him **outside** for a walk.
雪倫帶牠去外面散步。

parking lot 停車場 ★★★★★

句型

» Tom drove around the **parking lot** looking for a good spot.
湯姆在停車場轉了又轉，想找個好位子。

» The **parking lot** near the department store was extremely expensive.
靠近百貨公司的停車場非常貴。

會話

A Where should I park my car?
我車該停哪裡？

B We have an underground **parking lot** beneath the hotel.
我們旅館有一個地下停車場。

passenger 乘客

句型

» Mary sat in the **passenger** seat while Tom drove the car.
當湯姆開車時，瑪麗坐在乘客位上。

» All the **passengers** on the airplane died in the accident.
飛機上所有乘客都死於這場意外中。

會話

A Your attention please. Would **passenger** Johnson please report to the ticket office?
注意，乘客強森先生，麻煩到票務中心一下。

B That's me. I wonder if there is a problem with my flight.
我就是，難道我的班機出什麼問題了嗎？

scooter 摩托車 ★★★★★

» Don't forget to put on your helmet when you take your **scooter**.
當你騎摩托車時，別忘了要帶安全帽。

» A **scooter** uses less gas than a car.
摩托車耗的油比車子少。

會話

A Are you going to buy a car?
你要買車嗎？

B No, I can't afford it. I'm going to get a **scooter** instead.
沒有，我負擔不起，我要買一部摩托車。

supermarket 超市 ★★★★★

» Jack did his grocery shopping at the **supermarket**.
傑克到超市買東西。

» The coffee is in aisle 4 of the **supermarket**.
咖啡在超市的第四排。

會話

A We need to go to the bakery, the deli, and the fish store.
我們需要去一趟麵包店、熟食店還有魚店。

B Why, when we can find all we need at the **supermarket**?
為什麼？我們要的，超市都有啊。

taxi 計程車 ★★★★★

句型

» Jack doesn't have a car so he takes a taxi everywhere.
傑克沒有車，所以去哪裡都搭計程車。

» The taxi driver asked us where we'd like to go.
計程車司機問我們想去哪裡。

會話

A Should we take the public transportation?
我們要搭乘大眾運輸工具嗎？

B No. A taxi is much quicker.
不，計程車比較快。

temple 寺廟 ★★★★★

句型

» The monks and nuns were praying in the temple.
和尚和尼姑都在廟裡拜拜。

» We visited a Buddhist temple in Thailand.
我們在泰國時，造訪了一間佛教寺廟。

會話

A Where is the music coming from?
那個音樂從哪來的？

B It's coming from the temple down the road. Today is an important day for Taoists.
從路那頭的寺廟傳來的，今天是道教的重大日子。

through 透過

句型

» Jack walked **through** the door and into the hall.
傑克穿過門，走到了走廊。

» Let's take a shortcut **through** the building.
走那條穿過建築物的捷徑吧。

會話

A Should we drive **through** the city center?
我們應該開過市中心嗎？

B No. I think it's best if we drive around it.
不要，我想最好還是繞過市中心比較好。

toward 向……靠近

句型

» The bull slowly moved **toward** the matador.
那頭牛緩慢地向鬥牛士靠近。

» Jack walked **toward** the river, to get some fresh air.
傑克走向河邊，呼吸新鮮空氣。

會話

A Are you headed **toward** London?
你要去倫敦嗎？

B Yes, but we're only going as far as Oxford.
是的，但我們目前只走到牛津。

train station 火車站 ★★★★★

句型

» What time does your train arrive at the **train station**?
你的火車何時會進站？

» The **train station** was packed with people leaving town.
火車站被要出城的人們擠得水洩不通。

會話

A Where are you going with that luggage?
你拿那個行李箱要去哪裡？

B To the **train station.** I'm catching a train to Paris this afternoon.
去火車站。我要搭今天下午的火車去巴黎。

travel 旅行 ★★★★

句型

» Tom has **traveled** all over the world.
湯姆已經環遊過全世界了。

» I prefer **traveling** by train to **traveling** by bus or plane.
比起搭巴士或飛機旅行，我比較喜歡搭火車旅行。

會話

A Do you **travel** much?
你常旅行嗎？

B Not really. I'd rather stay at home during my holidays.
並沒有。在假日時，我寧可待在家裡。

turn (v.) 轉向 ★★★★★

句型

» Turn left at the corner to reach the video store.
在轉角向左轉，就可以到錄影帶店了。

» Lisa turned around in her seat to talk to the girl behind her.
麗莎在座位上轉身，和後面的女生說話。

會話

A I can't open the door!
我打不開門！

B You're turning the handle the wrong way. Turn it counterclockwise.
你把門把轉錯方向了，要逆時針方向轉。

turn (n.) 轉彎處 ★★★★★

句型

» At the next turn, go left.
在下一個轉彎處，左轉。

» Be careful. There's a turn in the road up ahead.
小心，在這條路的前方有個彎。

會話

A Should we go straight through this intersection?
要直走過十字路口嗎？

B Yes. Then, go right at the next turn.
是的，然後在下一個轉彎時右轉。

turn (n.) 輪到某人 ★★★★★

句型

» After Jack, it was Mary's **turn** to go next.
在傑克後，下一個輪到瑪麗。

» Whose **turn** is it to take out the garbage?
輪到誰把垃圾拿去倒？

會話

A This computer game is really fun.
這個電腦遊戲真的很好玩。

B Can I have a **turn**?
可以換我玩嗎？

U-turn 迴轉 ★★★★★

句型

» It's illegal to make **U-turns** in the middle of the street.
在路中央迴轉是違法的。

» Jack made a **U-turn** at the corner and went back in the other direction.
傑克在轉角處迴轉，然後往回走。

會話

A Oh no! We missed the turn.
不好了，我們錯過了那個轉彎。

B Make a **U-turn** up ahead.
在前面迴轉吧。

world 世界 ★★★★★

句型

» Bill Gates is the richest man in the **world**.
比爾・蓋茲是世界上最富有的人。

» Our **world** is made up of mostly carbon and hydrogen.
我們這個世界大多是由碳氣和氫氣組成。

會話

A Do you believe in aliens?
你相信有外星人嗎？

B Well, I think there must be some other life on other **worlds**.
呃，我相信其他世界裡一定有別的生物。

Chapter 6

Useful Verbs

常用動詞

Author's Note (作者的叮嚀)

Along with nouns, verbs are the most important words to know in the English language. After all, they provide the action of the sentences. However, because there are so many tenses in English, the verb endings often change. It's a good idea to know these endings in order to form grammatically correct sentences.

和名詞一樣，動詞是英文中最必要認識的字。畢竟，動詞為句子帶來動作。但是因為英文中有許多時態，動詞字尾常有變化，你最好知道這些字尾，以便造出文法正確的句子。

advise (v.) 勸告

句型

» The lawyer **advised** his client to plead guilty.
律師勸他的客戶認罪。

» I **advise** you to study English. It will be good for your future.
我勸你去學英文，這對你的未來有利。

A What should I do with this extra money?
多餘的錢要用來做什麼才好？

B I **advise** you to save it. You might need it for an emergency.
我勸你把它存起來，緊急狀況下，你也許會需要它。

advice (n.) 忠告，勸告 ★★★★★

句型

» Can I give you some **advice**? Open your own business.
我可以給你一些忠告嗎？你自己出來做老闆吧。

» Jack took the **advice** from his doctor and stayed home to rest.
傑克接受他醫生的忠告，待在家裡休息。

會話

A I think you should ask your boss for a raise in salary.
我認為你應該向老闆爭取加薪。

B That's good **advice**. I could use the extra money.
這建議不錯，我可以使用額外的錢。

allow 允許 

句型

» We are not **allowed** to smoke in this restaurant.
這間餐廳禁止吸煙。

» Allow me to introduce myself: My name is Darren.
容許我介紹我自己，我的名字是達倫。

會話

A Are dogs **allowed** in this park?
狗兒可以進這座公園嗎？

B Yes, but only if you have them on a leash.
可以，但你必須把牠們用狗練拴住才行。

argue 爭論 ★★★★★

句型

» Tom's parents got divorced because they always **argued** about money.
湯姆的父母離婚了，因為他們總是為錢爭吵。

» We were **arguing** so loudly, the neighbors complained.
我們吵得太大聲了，鄰居們都在抱怨。

會話

A But I don't want to clean the dishes!
但我不想洗碗！

B Don't **argue** with me, young lady! You'll do what I say.
小姐，不要和我吵。我說什麼，妳做什麼。

arrange 安排 ★★★★★

句型

» Lisa **arranged** the flowers so they looked pretty.
麗莎把花擺設的很美麗。

» Let's **arrange** a meeting for sometime next week.
下週找個時間，安排一個會議吧。

會話

A We should do something for Michael before he moves to America.
在麥可搬去美國之前，我們應該為他做些事。

B I know! Let's **arrange** a going-away party.
我知道！我們安排一個惜別會吧。

attack (v.) 攻擊 ★★★★★

句型

» The thief **attacked** the old woman and stole her purse.
小偷攻擊那個老婦人，並偷了她的皮包。

» Germany **attacked** Poland in 1939, starting World War II.
1939年德國攻打波蘭，開啟了第二次世界大戰。

會話

A What happened to your face? You have so many scars.
你的臉怎麼了？有好多疤痕。

B I was **attacked** by a dog in the street.
我昨晚在街上被狗攻擊。

attack (n.) 攻擊 

句型

» There's been a terrorist **attack** on The White House.
恐怖份子對白宮發動攻擊。

» The **attack** on Hiroshima was the first time atomic bombs were used.
原子彈首次使用是用於廣島之役上。

會話

A What's wrong? Your face is turning gray.
怎麼了？你的臉色好難看。

B I think I'm having a heart **attack**.
我想我的心臟病發了。

avoid 躲避

句型

» Lisa won't return my calls. I think she's **avoiding** me.
麗莎不回我電話，我想她在躲避我。

» Jack just barely **avoided** being hit by the car.
傑克差點躲不過那輛車子的衝撞。

會話

A Where's Paul? I get the feeling he's **avoiding** me.
保羅在哪裡？我覺得他好像在躲我。

B He probably doesn't want you to see him, because he hasn't finished the project yet.
他大概不想要你見到他，因為他還沒完成他的計畫。

beat 打；打敗

★★★★★

句型

» The old woman **beat** the thief over his head with her purse.
老婦人用皮包打那個小偷的頭。

» The Canadians **beat** the Americans 5-2 in the Olympic ice hockey match.
在奧林匹克冰上曲棍球賽中，加拿大以5比2擊敗美國。

會話

A I'm going to punch you in the mouth if you don't shut up.
如果你不閉嘴的話，我會用拳頭打你的嘴。

B If you do, I'll **beat** you with this stick.
如果你這樣做的話，我會用棍子打你。

cancel 取消 ★★★★★

句型

» The soccer match was **cancelled** due to rain.
足球賽因雨取消了。

» I'd like to **cancel** my membership to this club.
我想要取消我的俱樂部會員資格。

會話

A Are you still going to the theater tonight?
你今晚仍要去看戲嗎？

B Unfortunately not. The show was **cancelled** because the lead actor is ill.
大概不了，因為男主角生病，表演取消了。

chase 追趕 ★★★★★

句型

» The dog **chased** the cat down the street.
這隻狗追趕貓到街尾。

» The police were **chasing** after the man who robbed the bank.
警察緊追那個搶了銀行的男人。

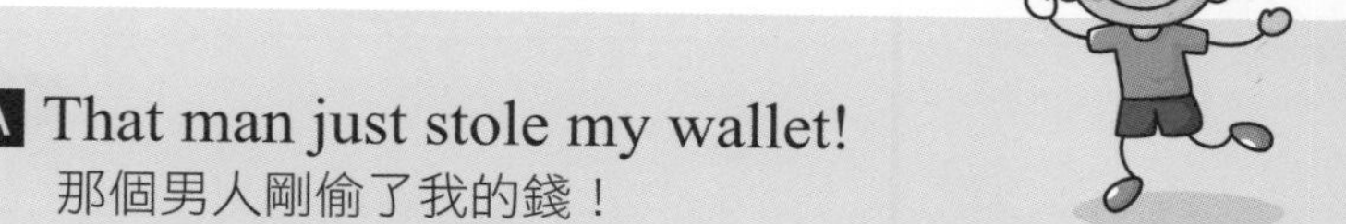

會話

A That man just stole my wallet!
那個男人剛偷了我的錢！

B Well, don't just stand there. Let's **chase** him.
不要只是站在那裡，一起追他呀。

cheat 作弊 ★★★★★

句型

» The teacher caught John **cheating** on his test.
老師逮到約翰在考試時作弊。

» Johnny likes to **cheat**. He hides cards up his sleeve.
強尼喜歡作弊，他玩牌時把牌藏在袖子裡。

會話

A Can I look at your answers?
我可以看你的答案嗎？

B Hey! That's **cheating**.
嘿！那是作弊！

choose 選擇 ★★★★★

句型

» I don't like the color of this jacket. Can I **choose** a different color?
我不喜歡這件夾克的顏色，可以選不同的顏色嗎？

» Jack must **choose** between a loving family and a successful career.
傑克必須在美滿家庭和成功事業之間作選擇。

會話

A I can't decide: I like both stereo systems.
我做不了決定，兩套音響我都喜歡。

B If you **choose** the more expensive one, you get a free CD.
如果你選較貴的那一套，你就可以得到一片免費CD。

congratulate 恭喜 ★★★★★

句型

» I'd like to **congratulate** you on passing your driving test.
我想要恭喜你通過路考。

» Mary **congratulated** her friend on her wedding day.
瑪麗在她朋友結婚那天去恭賀她。

會話

A My wife's going to have a baby!
我太太要生小孩了

B Let me be the first to **congratulate** you.
讓我第一個恭喜你。

continue 繼續 ★★★★★

句型

» I'm sorry I interrupted you. Please **continue** what you were saying.
很抱歉我打斷了你，請繼續說。

» After graduating from high school, Jack will **continue** his studies at a university.
在高中畢業後，傑克將繼續就讀大學。

會話

A Is the movie over? That can't be the end!
電影演完了嗎？結局怎麼會是這樣？

B It isn't. It's to be **continued** next week.
還沒結束，下週會繼續。

control (v.) 控制 ★★★★★

句型

» Engineers can **control** the satellite from the NASA headquarters.
工程師可以從太空總署控制衛星。

» Jack **controls** 25% of the company.
傑克控制了公司25%的股權。

會話

A Why is the car swerving all over the road?
為什麼這部車子在路上滑來滑去？

A I can't **control** the steering. We must have a flat tire.
我控制不了方向盤，一定是爆胎了。

control (n.) 控制 ★★★★★

句型

» The pilot lost **control** of the airplane and crashed into the sea.
飛機駕駛失去對飛機的控制，墜機撞進海裡了。

» Paul changed TV channels using a remote **control**.
保羅用遙控器轉台。

會話

A That man makes me so angry; I could throw something at him.
那個男人讓我好生氣，我想用東西丟他。

B **Control** yourself. He's leaving soon.
控制你自己，他馬上就會走了。

decrease 降低 ★★★★★

句型

» Because of the bad economy, the value of the dollar has **decreased**.
因為經濟不景氣，錢就貶值了。

» There's been a **decrease** in crime since that man was elected.
在那個男人當選後，犯罪降低了。

會話

A I'm coughing all the time.
我老是一直咳嗽。

A You should **decrease** the number of cigarettes you smoke.
你應該降低抽煙的數量。

defend 捍衛；辯護 ★★★★★

句型

» The tall, stone walls were built to help **defend** the fortress.
那個高聳的石牆是建來捍衛堡壘的。

» When the thief attacked, Jack threw his arms up to **defend** himself.
當小偷攻擊時，傑克揚起手來保護他自己。

會話

A Are you nervous about going to court tomorrow?
明天要上法庭，你會緊張嗎？

B Not really. I have a good lawyer **defending** my case.
不會，我有一個好律師，辯護我的案子。

dial (v.) 撥號 ★★★★★

» Jack **dialed** the phone number to the police station.
傑克撥電話到警察局。

» If you're lonely, **dial** up a friend.
如果你寂寞的話，打電話找朋友。

會話

A Where can we find good take-out Pizza?
哪裡有好吃的外帶披薩？

B Just **dial** 882-5252.
打882-5252這個電話就可以了。

dial (n.)（電話、電視的）按鍵盤；（收音機的）刻度盤★★★★★

句型

» Would you turn down the **dial** on the TV? It's too loud.
你可不可以把電視音量調低，太大聲了。

» The **dial** on this radio is stuck.
收音機的刻度盤卡住了。

會話

A Why is your telephone **dial** so big?
你的電話轉盤怎麼這麼大？

B Because I have fat fingers.
因為我的手指很粗啊。

feed 餵食 ★★★★★

句型

» Would you please **feed** the baby? She's crying for her bottle.
拜託你餵一下寶寶吧！她哭著想要喝奶。

» Jack likes **feeding** breadcrumbs to the birds in the park.
傑克喜歡在公園裡拿麵包屑餵鳥。

會話

A Do you believe in giving foreign aid?
你相信應該進行對外援助嗎？

B Yes, but first we must try to **feed** the starving people in our own country.
是的，但我們應先提供食物給自己國家中正在捱餓的人。

fight 打架 ★★★★★

句型

» Tom and his sister were **fighting** over who gets the remote control.
湯姆和他妹妹正在打架，看誰可以搶到遙控器。

» The English and the French **fought** a war for over 100 years.
英國和法國打了一百多年的仗。

會話

A Where did you get that black eye?
你怎麼黑了一隻眼睛？

B I got into a **fight** at the ice hockey match.
我在冰上曲棍球賽中，和別人打了一架。

greet 問候；迎接

句型

» The hostess of the party **greeted** all the guests at the door.
宴會的女主人在門口迎接賓客。

» **Greetings**! My name is Tom. Let me shake your hand.
你好！我是湯姆， 容許我和你握手。

會話

A I'm nervous about meeting your parents.
要見你的父母，我覺得很緊張。

B Just relax. When they open the door, **greet** them with a smile.
放輕鬆，當他們開門時，以笑容迎接他們。

guess 猜猜看

句型

» **Guess** how many fingers I'm holding behind my back.
猜猜我背後比幾根手指？

» Jack didn't know the answer so he **guessed**.
傑克不知道答案，所以就用猜的。

會話

A I wonder why John didn't come tonight.
我在想為什麼約翰今晚沒來。

B I **guess** he had better things to do.
我猜他有更好的事要做。

hang 掛

★★★★★

句型

» The picture is **hanging** on the wall.
畫掛在牆上。

» Children love to **hang** from monkey bars.
孩子們喜歡玩吊單槓。

會話

A What should I do with your keys?
我要怎麼處理你的鑰匙？

B Could you **hang** them on the back of the door, please?
把它們掛在門後，好嗎？

imagine 想像

句型

» Can you **imagine** what life would be like without music?
你能夠想像沒有音樂的人生會是怎樣嗎？

» In his office, Jack **imagined** he was on a beach somewhere warm.
傑克在辦公室裡，想像自己正在某處溫暖的海灘上。

會話

A I'm going to bring an umbrella to the park.
我要帶雨傘去公園。

B Ok, but I don't **imagine** we'll need it. Look how sunny it is.
好啊，但我想我們應該不需要，看看外面，陽光普照。

include 包括

句型

» Tax was not **included** in the price of the ticket. We had to pay extra.
票價中不含稅，我們還得要另外付稅。

» I **included** a greeting card with Harry's birthday gift.
我在哈利的生日禮物中，附了一張賀卡。

會話

A The price of the room is $50 dollars a night.
這個房間的價格是一晚五十美元。

B Does that **include** breakfast?
那包含早餐嗎？

increase 增加

句型

» They **increased** the price of gas. It's more expensive now.
他們調漲了油價，現在汽油更貴了。

» There's been a steady **increase** in the world population over the past 50 years.
在過去五十年中，世界人口一直穩定增加。

會話

A It looks like a storm is coming.
看起來，暴風雨要來了。

B I think you're right. The wind has **increased**.
我想你說的沒錯，風變大了。

introduce 介紹 ★★★★★

句型

» Jack **introduced** his new girlfriend to his parents.
傑克將新女友介紹給他爸媽。

» She **introduced** the new product with a short presentation.
她用很短的簡報介紹了新產品。

會話

A Lisa looks lonely lately.
麗莎最近看起來很寂寞。

B Maybe we should **introduce** her to one of your single friends.
也許我們應該把她介紹給你其中之一的單身朋友。

invite 邀請 ★★★★★

句型

» We **invited** 50 guests to the party.
我們邀請了五十位賓客參加宴會。

» Linda **invited** her parents over for dinner on the weekend.
琳達在週末時，邀請她父母過來吃晚餐。

A Why didn't Bob come to the party tonight?
為什麼鮑伯沒來今晚的舞會？

B Oops! I forgot to **invite** him.
完了，我忘了邀請他。

join 參加；加入 ★★★★★

句型

» Michael invited John to **join** their business club.
麥可邀請約翰加入他們的商業俱樂部。

» Hi, Bob! Would you like to **join** us for a drink?
嗨，鮑伯，要不要加入我們，一起喝一杯？

會話

A Are you guys playing a card game?
你們這些人在玩牌嗎？

B Yes. Would you like to **join** in? Pull up a chair.
是的，你想要加入嗎？拉一把椅子吧。

lay 放置 ★★★★★

句型

» Would you please **lay** the book down on the bed?
請你把書放在床上，好嗎？

» If you **lay** one hand on me, I'll scream.
如果你的手碰到我，我就尖叫。

會話

A What should I do with the ladder?
我要怎樣處理梯子呢？

B Just **lay** it down on the floor for now.
先把它放在地板上好了。

let 讓 ★★★★★

句型

» Would you please **let** the dog in?
你可以讓狗進來嗎？

» The teacher won't **let** us talk in class.
老師禁止我們在課堂上講話。

會話

A I can't lift these suitcases on my own.
我提不動這些行李箱。

B **Let** me help you.
我來幫你吧。

lie 躺 ★★★★★

句型

» Can I please **lie** down on a bed? I'm not feeling well.
我可不可以躺在床上？我覺得不太舒服。

» Tom **lay** down on the couch to watch television.
湯姆躺在長椅上看電視。

會話

A Where's Lisa?
麗莎在哪裡？

B She's **lying** down in her bedroom.
她正躺在她的臥房裡。

lie 說謊 ★★★★★

句型

» Phillip **lied** about his work experience in order to get the job.
菲力普為了要得到那份工作，謊報他的工作經驗。

» You're **lying** to me! I don't believe a word you say.
你在對我說謊！你說的話，我一個字都不信。

會話

A Did you really win the lottery?
你真的贏樂透了嗎？

B Would I **lie** to you? I swear I'm telling the truth.
我會對你說謊嗎？我發誓我說的是真的。

lift 提起；順便搭載 

句型

» These bags are heavy. Could you help me **lift** them up the stairs?
這些袋子好重，可以幫我把它們拿到樓上嗎？

» Paul hurt his back trying to **lift** some boxes.
保羅在提一些箱子時，傷到他的背。

會話

A I need to go to the doctor's office downtown.
我要去市中心醫生的看診室。

B Can I give you a **lift**? My car is just around the corner.
我可以載你一程嗎？我的車子就在轉角。

mind (v.) 介意 ★★★★★

句型

» Do you **mind** if I ask you a personal question?
你介不介意我問你一個私人問題？

» Jack doesn't **mind** lending money to people. He's happy to help.
傑克不介意把錢借給他人，他很樂意助人。

會話

A Do you **mind** if I smoke in here?
你介意我在這裡抽煙嗎？

B Yes, I do. Sorry, but I'm allergic to smoke.
是的，我介意。很抱歉，我對煙會過敏。

mix 混合 ★★★★★

句型

» Jack **mixed** all the cake ingredients in a bowl.
傑克將做蛋糕的材料，全部混在一個碗裡。

» I don't like to **mix** business with pleasure.
我不喜歡將公事和玩樂混為一談。

會話

A What happens when I **mix** red and yellow paint together?
我把紅色和黃色的油漆混在一起時，會怎樣？

B I think you'll get orange.
我想油漆會變成橘色。

need 需要 

句型

» All living things **need** water to survive.
所有生物都需要水，才能生存。

» Mary **needs** a new computer, because her old one broke down.
瑪麗需要一台新電腦，因為她的舊電腦壞了。

會話

A Is there something wrong, sir?
先生，有什麼問題嗎？

B I **need** a doctor. My friend is very sick.
我需要醫生，我朋友病得很重。

own 擁有 ★★★

» Do you **own** this house, or are you just renting it?
你擁有這棟房子嗎？還是你租的？

» Michael used to **own** a Porsche, but he sold it.
麥可以前有一部保時捷，但他賣掉了。

會話

A This essay should be typed.
這篇作文應該用打字的。

B But I don't **own** a computer or a typewriter.
但是我沒有電腦或打字機。

plant (v.) 種植 ★★★★★

句型

» We **planted** trees to rebuild the forests.
我們種樹，以重新建林。

» Lisa likes to **plant** roses in her front yard.
麗莎喜歡在她的前院裡種玫瑰。

會話

A Could you **plant** these seeds in the garden?
你可以把這些種子種在花園裡嗎？

B Sure. Do you have a shovel?
當然可以，你有鏟子嗎？

plant (n.) 植物 ★★★★★

句型

» Katie waters the house **plants** once a week.
凱蒂一個禮拜替室內盆栽澆一次水。

» **Plants** need a lot of sunshine to grow.
植物需要許多陽光，才能成長。

會話

A What kind of **plant** is this?
這是什麼植物？

B It's a fern, I think.
我想這是羊齒植物。

pollute 污染 ★★★★★

句型

» If we keep **polluting** the rivers, we'll have nothing but dirty water to drink.
如果我們繼續污染河川，我們將會只剩下骯髒的水可喝。

» It's a $500 fine for **polluting** in national parks.
污染國家公園，要罰500美元。

會話

A Would you throw this bottle out the window?
你可以把這瓶罐子丟到窗外嗎？

B That's **polluting**! Put it in a bag until we find a garbage can.
那是污染行為，在找到垃圾桶前，先把它放在袋子裡吧。

print 用印刷體寫；印製 ★★★★★

句型

» Billy **printed** the letters of his name on the blackboard.
比利把他名字的字母，用印刷體寫在黑板上。

» I have this file on my computer, but I need to **print** it out on paper.
我電腦上有這個檔案，但我需要把它列印出來。

會話

A Please **print** your essays double-spaced on white paper.
將你的作文印在白紙上，行距請空雙行。

B I can't. My printer is broken.
我做不到，我的印表機壞了。

promise 承諾 ★★★★★

句型

» Jack **promised** to love his wife until the day she died.
傑克承諾會愛他的妻子一生一世。

» **Promise** me you won't tell anyone my secret.
答應我，你不會把我的秘密告訴其他人。

會話

A Don't stay out late tonight.
今晚不要在外頭待太晚。

B I **promise** I'll be home before 10:00 pm.
我保證會在晚上十點以前到家。

protect 保護 ★★★★★

句型

» These sunglasses will **protect** my eyes from the bright sun.
這些太陽眼鏡會保護我的眼睛，不受烈陽的傷害。

» We need to **protect** our children from dangerous criminals.
我們需要保護我們的孩子，不受危險罪犯的傷害。

會話

A That man is coming after me with a gun!
那個男人拿著一把槍追我。

B Stand back. I'll **protect** you.
站在我後面，我會保護你。

quit 停止；戒掉 ★★★★★

句型

» Ever since Jack **quit** smoking, he feels a lot healthier.
自從傑克戒煙後，他覺得自己健康多了。

» **Quit** making all that noise! The neighbors will complain.
停止製造那些噪音！鄰居們會抱怨。

會話

A I'm thinking of **quitting** school.
我想要輟學。

B If you do that, you'll regret it for the rest of your life.
如果你這樣做的話，你這一輩子都會後悔。

receive 接到；收到 

句型

» William **received** a letter in the mail.
威廉收到一封信件。

» Lisa and Jack **received** many gifts on their wedding day.
琳達和傑克在結婚那天，收到許多禮物。

會話

A Do you **receive** a pension?
你會收到退休金嗎？

B Not until I turn 65 years old.
要等到我六十五歲時才會。

recycle 回收 ★★★★★

句型

» Jack **recycles** his old newspapers.
傑克回收舊報紙。

» I hope this city has a **recycling** program. There's no more room to dump garbage.
我希望這個城市有回收計畫，已經沒有空間可以倒垃圾了。

會話

A You have so many **recycling** bins.
你有這麼多回收筒。

B I know. This one is for plastic, this one for glass, and this one for paper.
我知道，這個回收塑膠、這個回收玻璃、這個回收紙類。

refuse 拒絕 ★★★★★

句型

» Jack was offered money from his parents, but he **refused**. He didn't need it.
傑克的父母要給他錢，但他拒絕了。他不需要這筆錢。

» I **refuse** to answer your rude questions.
我拒絕回答你無禮的問題。

會話

A Did your boss give you a promotion?
你老闆給你升遷嗎？

B He offered it, but I **refused**. I think I'm going to find a different job.
他提供了升遷機會，但我拒絕了。我想我會換個工作。

remind 提醒

句型

» In case I forget to lock the door, could you **remind** me?
如果我忘了鎖門，你可以提醒我嗎？

» Lisa **reminded** her husband that they had to go to a dinner party.
麗莎提醒她先生，他們得去參加一個晚宴。

會話

A **Remind** me to wash the car tomorrow.
提醒我明天要洗車。

B You're so forgetful. Must I **remind** you of everything?
你怎麼這麼健忘？我一定要每件事都提醒你嗎？

return 回到；退回 ★★★★★

句型

» The murderer **returned** to the scene of the crime.
殺人犯回到犯罪現場。

» We bought a **return** flight to Rome.
我們買了回羅馬的回程機票。

會話

A Could you **return** the movie to the video store for me? It's already 2 days late.
你可以幫我把錄影帶還給錄影帶店嗎？已經晚了兩天。

B Sure. I'll take it back on my way home from work.
當然可以，我在下班回家的路上會幫你還。

shut 關上 ★★★★★

句型

» Could you **shut** the window? It's getting cold in here.
你能不能關上窗子？屋裡變冷了。

» **Shut** that music off! It's starting to annoy me.
把音樂關掉！它讓我感到很煩。

會話

A Don't forget to **shut** the door on your way out.
離開時別忘了關門。

B I won't. If I leave it open, a thief might walk in.
我不會忘記的。如果忘了關，小偷可能會進來。

support 支持 ★★★★★

句型

» Michael **supported** his son's decision to travel the world.
麥可支持他兒子去環遊世界的決定。

» Dan's parents financially **supported** him all through university.
丹的父母給予他財務上的支持，讓他念完大學。

會話

A What are you going to do now that you're out of a job?
你現在沒工作，要怎麼辦呢？

B My husband is doing well, so I'm sure he can **support** the two of us for a while.
我先生的工作很穩定，我相信他可以暫時支撐兩個人的開銷。

surprise (v.) 給……驚喜 ★★★★★

句型

» We **surprised** Karen with flowers on her birthday.
在凱倫生日時，我們用送花給她驚喜。

» **Surprise**! I bought you a new car!
驚喜吧！我買了一部新車給你。

會話

A You're home early. I didn't expect you until 5:00 pm.
你回來早了，我以為要到五點才會看到你。

B I thought I'd **surprise** you. I got off work early.
我想給你一個驚喜，所以早點下班。

surprise (n.) 驚喜 ★★★★★

句型

» We threw Sam a **surprise** birthday party.
我們幫山姆開了一個驚喜派對。

» I don't like **surprises**. I always want to know what's going to happen.
我不喜歡驚喜，我希望知道會發生什麼事情。

會話

A What's in the box?
盒子裡有什麼東西？

B It's a **surprise**. You'll have to wait until Christmas.
這是一個驚喜，你得要等到聖誕節才會知道。

surprised (adj.) 驚訝的 ★★★★★

» Did you see the **surprised** look on Jack's face when he heard the good news?
當傑克聽到這個好消息時，你看到他臉上的驚訝表情了嗎？

» I'm not **surprised** John didn't come. He was feeling sick all week.
約翰沒來，我並不驚訝，他整個星期都不太舒服。

會話

A Oh my! Did you make dinner for all of us?
噢！天啊！你為大家準備了晚餐嗎？

B Don't look so **surprised**. I love to cook for people.
不要這麼驚訝，我喜歡做菜給別人吃。

thank 謝謝 ★★★★★

» I'd like to **thank** you for the gift. It was very considerate.
謝謝你送給我的禮物，你很貼心。

» The new president **thanked** the people who voted for him.
新總統感謝那些投票給他的人。

會話

A I brought flowers.
我帶來了一些花。

B **Thank** you very much. They're beautiful.
很感謝你，它們很美。

trust 信任 ★★★★★

句型

» Jack doesn't **trust** politicians. He thinks they often lie.
傑克不信任政客，他認為他們常常說謊。

» Do you **trust** me enough to take care of the baby?
你信任我幫你照顧寶寶嗎？

會話

A I'm not sure if your plan is a good idea.
我不確定你的計畫是不是個好主意。

B **Trust** me. I know what I'm doing.
相信我，我知道我在做什麼。

try 嘗試 ★★★★★

句型

» Karen **tried** talking to her parents, but they wouldn't listen.
凱倫試著和她的父母溝通，但他們就是不聽。

» We **tried** a new restaurant last week.
我們上週嘗試了一家新餐廳。

會話

A You have to do better in school.
你得再用功一點。

B I'm **trying** really hard, but I just can't seem to improve my grades.
我已經很努力了，但是我似乎就是改善不了我的成績。

want 想要 ★★★★★

句型

» Do you **want** anything to drink or eat?
你想要什麼吃的或喝的東西嗎？

» Jack **wanted** to go on vacation, but he had to work.
傑克想要去度假，但他得要工作。

會話

A Let's go to a movie.
一起去看電影吧。

B I don't **want** to see a movie. I'd rather stay home.
我不想要看電影，我寧願待在家裡。

wish 希望（較不可能達成的希望） ★★★★★

句型

» I **wish** I had a million dollars.
我希望我有一百萬美元。

» If you **wish** upon a star, all your dreams will come true.
如果你對星星許願，所有你的夢想都會實現。

會話

A If it wasn't for this weather, we could go to the park.
如果天氣不是這樣的話，我們就可以去公園了。

B I know. I **wish** it would stop raining.
我知道，我希望雨可以停。

worry 擔心 ★★★★★

句型

» Tom **worries** about his children's future.
湯姆擔心他孩子的未來。

» I can't sleep. I'm **worried** about my test tomorrow.
我睡不著，我擔心明天的考試。

會話

A Don't you think we should call Melissa? She should be here by now.
你認為我們應該打電話給瑪莉莎嗎？她現在早就該到了。

B Don't **worry**. I'm sure she's just running late.
別擔心，我確定她只是遲到了。

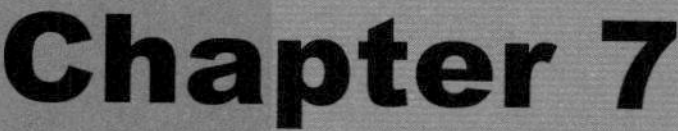

Chapter 7

Must-Know Nouns

不可不知的名詞

Author's Note (作者的叮嚀)

If verbs provide the action to sentences, then nouns are the words performing those actions. You might say that nouns are the most essential part of the sentence. Nouns come in two forms. If they are doing the action, they are "subjects". If the action is being done to them, they are "objects".

如果動詞是句子的動作，名詞就是執行這些動作的詞。你或許可以說，名詞是句子最重要的一部分。名詞有兩種形式，如果他們是執行動作者，他們便是「主詞」，如果他們是動作的承受者，那他們便是「受詞」。

accident 意外 ★★★★★

句型

» There was an **accident** between two cars on the highway, but no one was hurt.
高速公路上，兩部車子發生了車禍，但沒人受傷。

» Sorry, I didn't mean to step on your toe. It was an **accident**.
抱歉，我不是故意要踩你的腳，這是個意外。

會話

A Why is there salt all over the floor?
地板上為什麼都是鹽？

B I knocked it off the table by **accident**.
我不小心把它從桌上碰撞到地上了。

age 年齡 ★★★★★

句型

» If I had to guess at Jack's **age**, I'd say he was about 30 years old.
如果我必須要猜傑克的年紀，我會說他大概是三十歲。

» Please fill in your **age** and gender on the forms.
請把你的年齡、性別填到表中。

會話

A My son is always in trouble at school.
我兒子總是在學校裡惹麻 。

B He's at that **age** where boys like to rebel.
他現在正處於男孩們叛逆的年紀。

ant 螞蟻 ★★★★★

句型

» **Ants** are very hardworking insects.
螞蟻是非常辛勤工作的昆蟲。

» The red **ants** bite, but the black ones don't.
紅螞蟻會咬人，但黑色的不會。

會話

A It's a perfect day for a picnic.
今天的天氣適合郊遊。

B It'd be even better if there weren't so many **ant** hills around.
如果沒有這麼多螞蟻窩，會更好。

blood 血 ★★★★★

句型

» Oh my God! There's **blood** on your face. Were you in a fight?
天啊！你臉上有血，你和人打架了嗎？

» Jack's **blood** type is AB positive.
傑克的血型是AB型陽性。

會話

A Will Lisa be all right?
麗莎沒問題吧？

B I'm not sure. She lost a lot of **blood** in the accident.
我不確定，她在車禍中失了很多血。

captain 船長 ★★★★★

句型

» The **captain** of the ship is dining with us this evening.
這艘船的船長今晚要和我們共進晚餐。

» Tom's the number one player. He's the **captain** of the hockey team.
湯姆是一號球員，他是曲棍球隊的隊長。

會話

A Excuse me, Miss. Can you tell me when we'll be landing?
小姐，抱歉。你可以告訴我降落的時間嗎？

B I'll go ask the **captain** of the plane.
我去問一下機長。

century 世紀 ★★★★★

句型

» A lot can happen in a **century**. One hundred years is a long time.
一世紀中可以發生很多事，一百年是很長的時間。

» Leonardo da Vinci was born in the 15th **century**.
達文西出生於十五世紀。

會話

A When did the First World War begin?
第一次世界大戰什麼時候開始？

B At the beginning of last **century**. In 1914.
上個世紀初，1914年。

channel 頻道 ★★★★★

句型

» Please turn the TV to **channel** 5. There's a tennis match on.
將電視轉到第五頻道，現在正在播網球賽。

» Discovery is my favorite TV **channel**. I just love the animal programs.
「探索頻道」是我最喜歡的電視頻道，我喜歡看有關動物的節目。

會話

A Are you watching the news? The president has just been killed.
你在看新聞嗎？總統剛剛被殺了。

B Oh my! What **channel** is it on?
天啊！是哪個頻道？

choice 選擇 ★★★★★

» You have two **choices**: Take the bus or walk.
你有兩個選擇：搭公車或走路。

» Karen had to make a **choice** between buying a new car and going on vacation.
凱倫必須做選擇，是要買新車還是去度假？

會話

A Are you working late tonight?
你今晚要加班嗎？

B I don't have a **choice.** This project needs to be done by tomorrow.
我沒選擇。這計畫明天要完成。

crime 犯罪 ★★★★★

» The rate of **crime** has increased over the past 5 years.
犯罪率在過去五年中增加了。

» This is a safe neighborhood. There's practically no **crime**.
這附近很安全，幾乎沒有犯罪事件。

會話

A Did you know Jack was once in jail?
你知道傑克曾經坐過牢嗎？

B Really? What **crime** did he commit?
真的嗎？他犯了什麼罪？

crowd (n.) 群眾 ★★★★★

句型

» There was a **crowd** of people gathered around the door.
有一群人聚集在門口。

» Michael doesn't like **crowds**. With all those people, there's no space to move.
麥可不喜歡群眾。人這麼多，都沒有地方可以移動。

會話

A Can you see Paul anywhere?
你看得到保羅嗎？

B There he is! Among that **crowd** of people across the street.
他在那裡，在對街的人群中。

crowded (adj.) 擁擠的 

句型

» After school, the bus gets **crowded** with students.
放學後，因為學生，公車變得擁擠。

» It's too **crowded** in here. Can we go outside, where there's more space?
這裡好擠，我們到外面去，好嗎？那裡空間比較大。

會話

A Let's go to Paris this year.
今年去巴黎吧。

B I don't know. Paris gets so **crowded** with tourists.
我不確定，巴黎因為觀光客而變得好擁擠。

damage 損壞 ★★★★★

句型

» After the accident, there was a lot of **damage** to Peter's car.
車禍後，彼得的車子被撞得很慘。

» The typhoon caused over a billion dollars worth of **damage**.
颱風導致超過十億的損害。

會話

A Your house will cost a fortune to fix.
你的房子要修理，需要花很多錢。

B Our insurance should cover the **damage**.
我們的保險應該涵蓋這些損失。

department 部門

句型

» Does he work in the sales **department**?
他在業務部工作嗎？

» That **department** store is having a huge sale this weekend.
百貨公司這個週末有大型拍賣會。

會話

A How do I apply for a passport?
我要如何申請護照？

B You need to go to the Foreign Affairs **Department**.
你需要去外交部。

distance 距離 ★★★★★

句型

» What's the **distance** between New York and Los Angeles?
紐約和洛杉磯之間，距離有多遠？

» Jack runs a **distance** of 2 kilomenters every day.
傑克每天跑兩公里的距離。

會話

A Do you know how far it is to the next city?
你知道到下一個城市有多遠嗎？

B The **distance** is only about 50 miles. You should be there in an hour.
距離只有五十英哩，你應該一個小時就可以到。

dolphin 海豚 

句型

» **Dolphins** will often follow ships in the ocean.
海豚常在海洋中跟隨船隻。

» Some scientists believe **dolphins** have their own language.
部分科學家相信海豚有自己的語言。

會話

A Oh, my Goodness! Is that a shark's fin near the shore?
天啊！在海岸邊的是鯊魚鰭嗎？

B No. I think it's only a **dolphin**.
不是，我想那只是一隻海豚。

email 電子郵件 ★★★★★

句型

» My **email** address is john.doe@hotmail.com.
我的電子郵件是john.doe@hotmail.com。

» Is there an Internet café near here? I have to check my **email**.
這附近有網咖嗎？我得要查我的電子郵件。

會話

A Could you get me those reports by Monday?
星期一那些報告可以給我嗎？

B Sure. I'll **email** them to you over the weekend.
當然，我會在週末時，以電子郵件傳給你。

energy 能源；精力 ★★★★★

句型

» After Jack ran around the block, he was out of **energy**.
在傑克繞著這一區跑完後，他渾身無力。

» Wind power is a renewable source of clean **energy**.
風力是一種可以重覆再生的乾淨能源。

會話

A Did you pay the **energy** bill this month?
你這個月付水電費了嗎？

B Yes, and it was quite high, since it's been so hot lately.
付了，因為最近很熱，帳單金額很高。

engine 引擎；消防車 ★★★★★

句型

» Jack opened the hood of the car to look at its **engine**.
傑克打開車子的前蓋，檢查引擎。

» We could hear the sirens of a fire **engine** down the street.
我們在街尾都可以聽到消防車的警報聲。

會話

A Are you going to the auto mechanic?
你要去修車技工那裡嗎？

B Yes. I need to change the **engine** oil in the car.
是的，我需要換車子的機油。

freedom 自由 

句型

» In a democracy, you have the **freedom** to say what you want.
在民主體系下，你有表達自己意見的自由。

» This dolphin has never experienced **freedom**. It's been in a zoo since it was born.
這隻海豚從未體驗過自由。牠從一出生，就一直待在動物園。

會話

A What was it like for the black slaves in America?
以前的黑奴在美國的生活如何？

B They didn't have the rights and **freedoms** white people did.
他們沒有白人所享有的權利和自由。

goal 目標 ★★★★★

» My **goal** is to make a million dollars by the time I'm 30.
我的目標是在三十歲前賺到一百萬元。

» The **goal** of the meeting was to find a way to decrease crime.
這次會議的目標是找到降低犯罪的方法。

會話

A What are your **goals** for the future?
你未來的目標是什麼？

B I hope to study medicine, get married, and write a book when I'm older.
我希望攻讀醫學，然後結婚，等到老一點時，再寫一本書。

government 政府 ★★★★★

» The United States of America has a democratically elected **government**.
美國政府是一個由民主政治選出的政府。

» Last year, the federal **government** cut taxes.
去年，聯邦政府減稅。

會話

A What does Karen do for a living?
凱倫的工作是什麼？

B She has a **government** job in the Department of Transportation.
她在交通部任公職。

height 高度；身高 ★★★★★

句型

» I need to know your **height**. Can I measure how tall you are?
我需要知道你的身高，可以幫你量量看嗎？

» The **height** of the building is 50 meters.
這棟建築物的高度是五十公尺。

會話

A You look like you've grown. What's your **height**?
你看起來長大了，身高多少？

B 5 feet, 4 inches. I'm almost as tall as my mother now.
五呎四吋，我現在幾乎和我媽一樣高了。

human 人類 ★★★★★

句型

» **Human** beings are different from other animals.
人類和其他動物不同。

» It's only **human** to make mistakes.
人非聖賢，孰能無過。

會話

A Do you think **humans** will be on Earth forever?
你認為，人類會永遠存活在地球上嗎？

B I don't think so. We'll probably end up like the dinosaurs.
我不認為，我們可能會和恐龍有相同的下場。

hunger (n.) 飢餓 ★★★★

» It's only natural for humans to feel **hunger** and thirst.
人類會感到飢餓、口渴，是很自然的事。

» Jack ate a cheeseburger to feed his **hunger**.
傑克吃了一個起士漢堡充飢。

會話

A That boy sure studies a lot.
那個男孩真的很用功。

B I guess you could say he has a **hunger** for learning.
我想你可以說他渴望學習。

insect 昆蟲 ★★★★

» Your house is full of **insects**: flies, spiders, ants, and cockroaches.
你的房子裡都是昆蟲，蒼蠅、蜘蛛、螞蟻和蟑螂都有。

» This spray protects fruits and vegetables from **insects**.
這個噴劑可以保護水果和蔬菜不受昆蟲侵害。

會話

A Have you ever heard of a centipede?
你曾聽過蜈蚣嗎？

B Isn't that an **insect** with one hundred legs?
那不是一種有一百隻腳的昆蟲嗎？

joke 笑話；開玩笑 ★★★★★

句型

» At the party, Jack told a funny **joke** and everyone laughed.
在舞會中，傑克說了一個很好笑的笑話，每個人都笑了。

» That comedian tells nothing but dirty **jokes**.
那個詼星只會說黃色笑話。

會話

A Here's the money I owe you.
這是我欠你的錢。

B Is this a **joke**? You owe me much more than this!
這是在開玩笑嗎？你欠我的不只這些！

kilogram 公斤 ★★★★★

句型

» Last time I checked, I weighed 65 **kilograms**.
我上一次測量時，我重六十五公斤。

» The oranges are $.50 per **kilogram**.
橘子是每公斤五十分錢。

會話

A I'm going shopping. Do you need anything?
我要去買東西，你需要什麼嗎？

B Yes. Could you please pick up 2 **kilograms** of flour?
是的，你可以買兩公斤的麵粉嗎？

kilometer 公里 ★★★★★

» The next city is 250 **kilometers** away.
下一個城市，距離這裡有二百五十公里。

» It's only a two-**kilometer** hike through the forest.
穿越這個森林，只有兩公里的路程。

會話

A How many miles in a **kilometer**?
一公里是幾英哩？

B There are 0.6 miles in every **kilometer**.
一公里等於零點六英哩。

maximum 最大值 ★★★★★

» This elevator can hold a **maximum** of 1100 kilograms.
這個電梯的最大載重是一千一百公斤。

» The **maximum** amount of people allowed in here is 100. No more than that.
這裡最多可容納一百人，不能再多了。

會話

A What will the repairs cost me?
修理費要花我多少錢？

B $200 **maximum**. I promise it won't be more.
最多二百元，我保證不會更多。

meaning 意義 ★★★★★

句型

» Paul couldn't understand the **meaning** of the question.
保羅不明白這個問題的意思。

» Do you know the **meaning** of the word, "maximum"? I've never heard it before.
你知道「最大值」這個詞的意思嗎？我以前從沒聽過這個詞。

會話

A What's the **meaning** of this? Why are all these people here?
這是什麼意思？為什麼這裡這麼多人？

B Surprise! We threw you a party!
給你個驚喜！我們為你辦了一個舞會！

minimum 最小值 ★★★★★

句型

» You must spend a **minimum** of $10 to eat at this restaurant.
這間餐廳的最低消費是十美元。

» The **minimum** age to vote in this country is 18.
這個國家的人民十八歲才有投票權。

會話

A Does it get very cold here in the winters?
這裡的冬天會很冷嗎？

B Not really. The **minimum** temperature is 5 degrees Celsius.
這倒不見得，最低溫度是攝氏五度。

mosquito 蚊子

句型

» A **mosquito** stung me and now my arm is really itchy.
蚊子咬了我，現在我的手臂真的很癢。

» Is it true that **mosquitoes** carry malaria?
蚊子會傳染瘧疾，是真的嗎？

會話

A Did you have trouble sleeping last night?
你昨晚睡不著嗎？

B Yes. I kept hearing the buzzing of a **mosquito** in my ear.
是的，我耳邊一直聽到蚊子的嗡嗡聲。

noise 噪音

句型

» Stop making so much **noise**! It's so loud in here I can't think.
停止製造這麼多噪音，這裡太吵，讓我無法思考。

» Your car is making a funny **noise**. Maybe you should get it fixed.
你的車子發出怪聲音，也許你應該修理一下。

會話

A Did you hear that strange **noise**?
你聽到那個奇怪的噪音了嗎？

B No. I can't hear anything but the wind.
沒有，我只聽到風的聲音。

peace 和平 ★★★★★

句型

» How can there be world **peace** if governments keep starting wars?
如果各國政府一直不斷開戰，怎麼可能有世界和平？

» I'm going to lie down. I need some **peace** and quiet from all this noise.
我要去躺一下，我需要遠離所有噪音，好好安靜一下。

會話

A Why is there so much fighting in the Middle East?
為什麼中東地區這麼多戰爭？

B I don't know. But both sides want **peace**.
我不知道，但他們雙方都想要和平。

pleasure 樂趣

句型

» Jack takes **pleasure** in helping people with their problems.
傑克以幫助人解決問題為樂。

» My name is Alex. It's a **pleasure** to meet you.
我的名字是艾力克斯，很高興見到你。

A Thank you for helping me move into my new apartment.
謝謝你幫我搬家到新的公寓。

B It was my **pleasure**. I'm always happy to help.
那是我的榮幸，我很樂意助人。

pollution 污染 ★★★★★

» Too many cars cause a lot of air **pollution**.
過多車輛造成許多空氣污染。

» This city is so clean. There's hardly any **pollution**.
這個城市好乾淨，幾乎沒有任何污染。

會話

A Is it safe to drink the water?
喝這個水，安全嗎？

B I wouldn't. The city has a problem with water **pollution**.
我才不喝，這個城市有水污染的問題。

population 人口 ★★★★★

» New York has a lot of people. The **population** is over 15 million.
紐約有許多人，其人口超過一千五百萬。

» The **population** of India is nearing one billion.
印度的人口接近十億。

會話

A What was the conference about?
這次的會議和什麼有關？

B We talked about the problem of growing urban **populations**.
我們談到城市人口增加所帶來的問題。

secret (n.) 秘密 ★★★★★

句型

» I'll tell you a **secret**. But you have to promise not to tell anyone else.
我告訴你一個秘密，但你要答應我不可以告訴其他人。

» Mary is not very good at keeping **secrets**.
瑪麗不擅於保密。

會話

A Do you have any **secrets** you've never told anyone?
你有任何從未告人的秘密嗎？

B Well, there is one. But I'm not telling you.
有一個，但我不會告訴你。

service 服務 ★★★★★

句型

» The **service** at this restaurant was terrible. I wouldn't tip.
這家餐廳的服務糟透了，我不會給小費的。

» Pull into that **service** station. We need gas.
開進那家服務站吧，我們需要加油。

會話

A Can I be of **service**, sir?
先生，我可以為您服務嗎？

B Yes. I'm looking for a double room for two nights.
是的，我需要一個雙人房，要待兩晚。

shrimp 蝦子 ★★★★★

» I love seafood. I especially like barbecued **shrimp**.
我喜歡海鮮，特別喜歡烤蝦。

» This restaurant is famous for its spicy **shrimp** soup.
這家餐廳以其辣蝦湯聞名。

會話

A What does Larry do for a living?
賴利是做什麼的？

B He's a fisherman. He mostly nets **shrimp** and lobster.
他是漁夫，大多捕蝦子和龍蝦。

smile (n.) 微笑 ★★★★★

» Lisa has a **smile** that lights up a room. She always looks so happy.
麗莎的微笑，可以讓整個房間亮起來，她看起來總是那麼快樂。

» Why are you frowning? Put a **smile** on your face.
你為什麼要皺眉？笑一個吧。

會話

A Have you ever seen the "Mona Lisa" in Paris?
你看過巴黎的「蒙娜麗莎的微笑」嗎？

B Yes. She has such a mysterious **smile**.
有，她有著神秘的笑容。

smile (v.) 笑 ★★★★★

句型

» What are you **smiling** at? Did someone tell you a joke?
你在笑什麼？有人告訴你笑話嗎？

» Jack **smiled** at the pretty woman across the room.
傑克對著房間那端的美女微笑。

會話

A Do you think Michael enjoyed the dinner?
你認為麥可喜歡這頓晚餐嗎？

B He's **smiling**, so he must've liked it.
他在微笑，應該是很喜歡吧。

thought 想法 ★★★★★

句型

» I just had a **thought**: Let's buy a new house.
我有一個想法，我們買新房子吧。

» My **thoughts** are with you on your wedding day.
你結婚那天，我會很想念你的。

會話

A Do you have any **thoughts** on our new clothing line?
你對新的服裝系列，有任何想法嗎？

B Well, I think the colors are a bit boring, but the style is great.
我認為顏色有些平凡，但款式很好。

trade (n.) 交易；貿易 ★★★★★

» Mary and Lisa switched lunches: They made a **trade**.
瑪麗和麗莎交換午餐，她們做了一個交易。

» Stockbrokers make **trades** every day on the stock market.
股票仲介每天都在股票市場中進行交易。

會話

A Why don't these two countries get along?
為什麼這兩個國家處不來？

B I think they have bad **trade** relations.
我想他們的貿易關係很糟。

trade (v.) 交換 ★★★★★

» Would you like to **trade** jackets? I like yours better.
你想交換夾克嗎？我比較喜歡你的。

» Paul **traded** in his truck for a brand new Volkswagen.
保羅用他的卡車，換了一台全新的福斯汽車。

會話

A Do you have any hobbies?
你有任何嗜好嗎？

B I like to **trade** baseball cards.
我喜歡和他人交換棒球卡。

trash 垃圾

★★★★★

句型

» Can you throw out the **trash**? It's starting to smell up the kitchen.
你可以把垃圾拿出去丟嗎？廚房開始發臭了。

» The **trash** collector picks up the garbage once a week.
垃圾車一週收一次垃圾。

會話

A What should I do with the leftover food from last week?
上週的剩菜剩飯，要如何處理？

B Just throw it in the **trash**, underneath the sink.
把它們丟進水槽下面的垃圾桶裡。

tunnel 隧道

句型

» This train went through a **tunnel** in the mountain.
這輛火車過了一個山洞。

» The bank robbers dug a **tunnel** underground to get into the bank.
銀行搶匪挖了一條隧道，進入銀行。

會話

A Why is it dark all of a sudden?
為什麼突然暗下來了？

B Don't worry, honey. We're just driving through a **tunnel**.
親愛的，別擔心，我們正開車經過隧道。

turkey 火雞 ★★★★★

句型

» Karen doesn't eat beef, pork, or chicken, but she loves turkey.
凱倫不吃牛肉、豬肉、或雞肉，但她愛死火雞了。

» Would you like me to make you a turkey sandwich?
你要我幫你做個火雞肉三明治嗎。

會話

A What sound does a turkey make?
火雞是怎樣叫的？

B You mean those ugly birds? Gobble, gobble, gobble.
你是說那些很醜的大鳥？牠們的叫聲是咯一咯一咯。

voice 聲音 

句型

» I can't hear your voice. Could you speak a little louder?
我聽不到你的聲音，可不可以說大聲一點？

» Jack has a loud voice. He always sounds like he's yelling.
傑克聲音很大，聽起來總是好像在吼人一樣。

會話

A Hi, Tom. How are you?
嗨，湯姆，你好嗎？

B Who is this? I don't recognize your voice.
你是誰？我認不出你的聲音。

wedding 婚禮 ★★★★★

句型

» After Jack proposed marriage to Lisa, they spent the next year planning the **wedding**.
在傑克向麗莎求婚後，他們次年一整年都在計畫婚禮。

» The bride and groom cut the **wedding** cake.
新郎和新娘切了婚禮蛋糕。

會話

A What are you doing this Saturday?
你這週六要做什麼？

B I'm going to a **wedding**. My cousin is getting married.
我要去參加婚禮，我表姊要結婚了。

weight (n.) 重量 ★★★★

句型

» Tom started eating less in order to keep his **weight** down.
為了要減重，湯姆開始少吃。

» The **weight** of this suitcase is 40 kilograms.
這個行李箱的重量是四十公斤。

會話

A Do you think I have a **weight** problem?
你認為我的體重有問題嗎？

B No, honey, you're just perfect: Not too thin and not too fat.
不，親愛的，你剛剛好，不會太瘦，也不會太胖。

weigh (v.) 稱……重 ★★★★★

» Randy **weighs** 160 pounds.
藍迪重一百六十磅。

» Please step on the scale to **weigh** yourself.
你站在體重計上秤重。

會話

A My Goodness, this bag is heavy. How much does it **weigh**?
我的天啊，這個袋子真重，它有多重？

B I'm not sure, but the airline charged me for the extra weight.
我不確定，但航空公司向我收了超重費用。

Chapter 8

Important Adjectives and Adverbs

重要的形容詞和副詞

Author's Note (作者的叮嚀)

Adjectives and adverbs provide flavor to nouns and verbs, the same way flowers will brighten up a room. Generally, adjectives describe nouns, and adverbs describe verbs and other adjectives. For many of the adjectives listed here, adding an "-ly" ending will make it an adverb.

形容詞和副詞為名詞和動詞加味，就像花朵使房間亮起來一樣。一般來說，形容詞形容名詞，副詞形容動詞和其他形容詞。下面列出的許多形容詞在加上ly後，就成了副詞。

almost (adj. / adv.) 幾乎

句型

» We're not quite finished our homework, but we're **almost** done.
我們還沒有做完功課，但幾乎差不多了。

» Jack **almost** missed the train. He had to run to catch it.
傑克差點趕不上火車，他得用跑的才趕得上。

會話

A Do you have any money left?
你有剩下任何錢嗎？

B **Almost** nothing. But I can lend you some if you need it.
幾乎沒有，但如果你需要，我可以借你一些。

alone (adj. / adv.) 一個人的（地）；獨自 ★★★★★

句型

» After all the guests left, Lisa was **alone** in the house.
在所有賓客離開後，麗莎獨自一人在屋裡。

» Leave me **alone**! I don't want to talk to anyone right now.
讓我一個人靜一下！我現在不想和任何人說話。

會話

A Do you live **alone**?
你一個人住嗎？

A No. I live with my sister and her boyfriend.
不，我和我姊和她男朋友一起住。

always (adv.) 總是 ★★★★★

句型

» Paul **always** drinks a cup of coffee in the morning.
保羅早上總是要喝杯咖啡。

» I don't **always** look this way. Normally, my hair is combed.
我平常看起來不是這樣，通常我頭髮會梳理整齊。

會話

A Do you **always** stay up this late?
你總是這麼晚睡嗎？

B No. Usually, I'm in bed before midnight, but I have to study for an exam.
不，通常我午夜之前就會上床，但我必須準備考試。

available (adj.) 有空的；可得到的 ★★★★★

» Do you have any rooms **available**?
你有任何空房嗎？

» The movie Karen wanted to rent wasn't **available**, so she picked a different one.
凱倫想要租的電影沒有，所以她挑了另一部片。

會話

A Let's set up a meeting. Are you **available** on Tuesday?
我們安排一個會議吧。你星期二有空嗎？

B Unfortunately not. Can we make it Wednesday instead?
沒有，換成星期三，好嗎？

basic (adj.) 基本的 ★★★★★

» Tom didn't care to learn the whole theory. He just wanted the **basic** idea.
湯姆不想學整個理論，他只想要知道基本概念。

» Just give me the **basic** facts.
只要給我基本的事實。

會話

A Do you live in a fancy apartment?
你住的公寓很漂亮嗎？

B No, it's really quite **basic**. I only have the essentials.
不，它很基本，只有一些基本配備。

colorful (adj.) 色彩豐富的 ★★★★★

句型

» What a **colorful** rainbow!
彩虹真是色彩鮮豔啊！

» This painting is very **colorful**: Reds, oranges, blues, greens...
這幅畫色彩豐富，有紅色、橘色、藍色、綠色……

會話

A What do you think of the new furniture?
你認為新家具如何？

B It's not very **colorful**. It's only black and white.
顏色太少，只有黑白兩色。

common (adj.) 共同的；常見的 ★★★★★

句型

» Mary and Irene are very different: They have nothing in **common**.
瑪麗和愛琳非常不同，她們沒有任何共同點。

» We sometimes get tornadoes in this area, but it's not very **common**.
我們這地區有時會有龍捲風，但不常見。

會話

A Do you also know Paul?
你也認識保羅？

B Yes. It looks like we have a **common** friend.
是的，看來我們似乎有個共同的朋友。

convenient (adj.) 便利的 ★★★★

句型

» The supermarket is four blocks away. That's not very **convenient**.
超市離這裡有四條街之遠，不是很便利。

» Our computer is so **convenient**: It's easy to use, and solves a lot of our problems.
我們的電腦非常方便，使用容易，解決我們很多問題。

會話

A Did you know that I work right across the street?
你知道我在對街工作嗎？

B How **convenient**! You can sleep late every morning.
真方便，你每天早上可以睡晚一點。

dangerous (adj.) 危險的 

句型

» Driving on the wrong side of the road is **dangerous**.
逆向行駛是很危險的。

» Jack has a **dangerous** job. He's a police officer.
傑克的工作很危險，他是警察。

會話

A Let's hitchhike across the country.
我們搭便車橫越美國吧！

B That's far too **dangerous**. It's safer to take a bus.
那太危險了，搭巴士比較安全。

dead (adj.) 死掉的

句型

» Peter's grandfather is not living anymore: He's **dead**.
彼得的祖父死了。

» There's a **dead** animal on the side of the road.
路邊有死掉的動物。

會話

A What happened? You look as though you've seen a ghost!
怎麼了？你看起來好像看到鬼了！

B I found a **dead** body by the river.
我在河邊發現了死屍。

different (adj.) 不同的

句型

» You look **different**. Have you lost weight?
你看起來很不同，瘦了很多嗎？

» Your apartment is **different** than ours. For one, yours is bigger.
你的公寓和我們的不同，其中一項是你的公寓較大。

會話

A I'll call you this evening.
我今晚會打電話給你。

B Wait, I have a **different** number now. I had to change it.
等一下，我現在的號碼不同了，我換掉舊號碼了。

foreign (adj.) 外國的 ★★★★★

句型

» Patricia likes to try **foreign** food for something different.
派翠西亞喜歡嘗試外國食物，品嚐不同的風味。

» Do you know where the **Foreign** Affairs Department is?
你知道外交部在哪裡嗎？

會話

A Mario speaks with an accent. Is he originally from here?
馬力歐說話有口音，他是這裡土生土長的嗎？

B No. I think he was born in a **foreign** country.
不是，我想他是在外國出生的。

interesting (adj.) 有趣的 ★★★★★

句型

» We watched an **interesting** program on TV last night.
昨晚我們在電視上看到一個很有趣的節目。

» Jack is an **interesting** man to talk to. He has many exciting stories.
傑克是很有趣的談話對象，他有許多很棒的故事。

會話

A Did you know that India was a British colony?
你知道印度以前是英國殖民地嗎？

B That's **interesting**! No wonder they can speak English.
那真有趣，難怪那裡的人會說英文。

lucky (adj.) 幸運的 ★★★★★

句型

» Jack is **lucky** when it comes to playing cards. He always wins.
傑克的牌運很好，他總是會贏。

» You're **lucky** you didn't lose your job after the way you talked to the boss.
在你那樣和老闆說話後，你沒丟掉工作真是幸運。

會話

A Did you hear the Joneses won a million dollars?
你聽說瓊斯一家人贏得一百萬元了嗎？

B **Lucky** them! What will they do with the money?
他們真是幸運，他們要怎樣用這筆錢呢？

main (adj.) 主要的 

句型

» The **main** street runs directly through town.
主街貫穿全鎮。

» The **main** entrance to the building has two revolving doors.
這棟大樓的主要入口有兩扇旋轉門。

會話

A What was the **main** point of his argument?
他主要的爭論點是什麼？

B I'm not sure. He talked in circles.
我不確定，他說話顛三倒四的。

minor (adj.) 次要的 ★★★★☆

句型

» We had a few minor problems, but nothing that important.
我們有幾個小問題，但都不是很重要。

» It's nothing serious. It's only a minor cut.
沒什麼嚴重的，只是小小割傷而已。

會話

A Did you hear that Jack was in the hospital?
你聽說傑克入院了嗎？

B Yes. I think he's having some minor surgery done.
是的，我想他要動一些小手術。

national (adj.) 國家的 

句型

» We caught a national flight from Sidney to Brisbane.
我們搭乘國內班機，從雪梨飛到布里斯本。

» The national animal of Canada is the beaver.
加拿大的國家代表動物是水獺。

會話

A Are you watching the news? Have they said anything about the Middle East?
你正在看新聞嗎？有沒有講到中東的事？

B This is the national news. The international news comes on at 6 pm.
這是國內新聞，國際新聞晚上六點開始。

negative (adj.) 負面的；不好的 ★★★★★

句型

» There is nothing **negative** I can say about him. I think he's perfect.
我對他沒有什麼負面評價，我認為他很完美。

» Jack's **negative** comments about the idea weren't welcome.
傑克對於這個想法的負面評價，不受大家的歡迎。

會話

A I'll never find a new job.
我永遠也找不到工作。

B Don't be so **negative**! Try to have a positive outlook on life.
不要這麼悲觀，試著對人生有正面看法。

private (adj.) 私人的 ★★★★★

句型

» Tom and Lisa were having a **private** conversation. No one else was meant to hear it.
湯姆和麗莎正在私下講話，沒有其他人應該聽到他們的談話。

» Jack doesn't talk much about his **private** life.
傑克不太常談論他的私人生活。

會話

A Could we go somewhere **private** to talk?
我們可以到別處去私下談話嗎？

B Sure. There's an empty room down the hall.
當然，走道底，有一間空房。

probably (adv.) 也許；可能 ★★★★★

句型

» It's **probably** going to rain on Monday, but no one knows for sure.
星期一可能會下雨，但沒有人可以確定。

» I'll **probably** retire when I'm 65, but I might work longer.
我在六十五歲時，可能會退休，但也可能再做久一點。

會話

A Are you coming for dinner on Friday?
你星期五要不要來共進晚餐？

B **Probably**. I'll have to see how much work I can get done this week.
也許，這得看看我這週可以做完多少工作。

rather (adv.) 寧願，寧可 ★★★★★

句型

» Emily walks to school, **rather** than taking the bus.
愛蜜莉走路去學校，而不願意搭公車。

» This place is **rather** cold. Could you turn up the heat?
這地方太冷了，你可以把暖氣打開嗎？

會話

A Would you like to try the fish?
你想吃點魚嗎？

B I'd **rather** have chicken, if you don't mind.
如果你不介意的話，我比較想吃雞肉。

responsible (adj.) 負責的 ★★★★★

句型

» Drinking and driving is not a **responsible** way to behave.
酒後駕車是不負責任的行為。

» Were you **responsible** for starting the fight?
你是不是那個要為引發這場架負責的人？

會話

A What exactly are your duties here?
你在這裡的職責究竟是什麼？

B I'm **responsible** for seeing that every guest is comfortable.
我負責確定每個賓客都感到很舒適。

seldom (adv.) 不常；很少 ★★★★★

句型

» We **seldom** have time to go to the movies. We're just too busy.
我們很少去看電影，我們太忙了。

» Tom always drives above the speed limit, but his wife **seldom** does.
湯姆總是超速，但他太太很少這樣子。

會話

A How often do you drink wine?
你多常喝酒？

B **Seldom**. I'm afraid I'm not much of a drinker.
幾乎不喝。我不是很會喝酒。

serious (adj.) 嚴肅的；嚴重的

句型

» Jack was **serious** about his job. He worked very hard.
傑克對工作很認真，他工作非常努力。

» There was a **serious** accident on the highway. Many people were killed.
在高速公路上發生一場重大車禍，造成許多人死亡。

會話

A I am really thinking of becoming a clown.
我真的很認真考慮要當小丑。

B Are you **serious**? I thought you were only joking.
你說真的嗎？我以為你只是在說笑。

sometimes (adj.) 有時候

句型

» Tom **sometimes** goes bowling, but not very often.
湯姆有時候會去打保齡球，但不常去。

» **Sometimes**, I like to treat myself to a fancy dinner in a restaurant.
有時候，我喜歡去餐廳享受高級的晚餐，以犒賞自己。

會話

A Do you ever listen to classical music?
你聽古典音樂嗎？

B **Sometimes**. But I prefer rock and roll.
有時候，但我比較喜歡搖滾樂。

special (adj.) 特別的 ★★★★★

句型

» This is a **special** watch. It can tell time all over the world.
這是支特別的錶，可以顯示世界各地的時間。

» Jack hopes to find a **special** woman he can spend the rest of his life with.
傑克希望找到一個特別的女人，共度一生。

會話

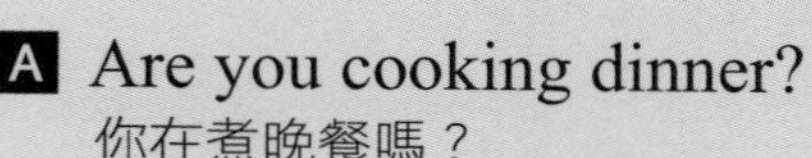

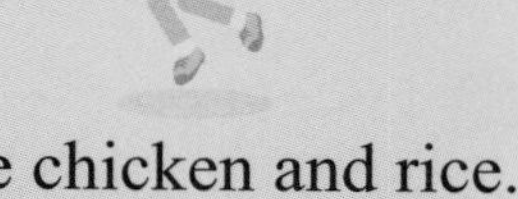

A Are you cooking dinner?
你在煮晚餐嗎？

B Yes, but nothing **special**. Just some chicken and rice.
是的，但沒什麼特別的，只是一些雞肉和米飯。

strange (adj.) 奇怪的 ★★★★★

句型

» There's a **strange** man standing outside the window. He keeps looking at me.
窗外站了一個奇怪的人，他一直看著我。

» This movie is **strange**. I don't understand any of it.
這部電影很奇怪，我完全看不懂。

會話

A Where's Karen? Did she leave already?
凱倫在哪裡？已經離開了嗎？

B That's **strange**. She was here just a minute ago.
這奇怪了，她一分鐘前還在這裡。

thick (adj.) 厚的 

句型

» This sandwich is so **thick** I can barely fit my mouth over it.
這個三明治太厚了，我嘴巴幾乎塞不進去。

» The **thickest** book Jack ever read was "War and Peace" by Tolstoy.
傑克讀過最厚的書是托爾斯泰寫的《戰爭與和平》。

會話

A What should we eat for dinner tonight?
我們今晚晚餐要吃什麼？

B I could go for a **thick**, juicy steak.
我們可以去吃一份肥厚、多汁的牛排。

unique (adj.) 獨特的；獨一無二的 

句型

» Peter is quite **unique**. I've never met anyone else like him.
彼得很獨特。我從來沒遇過像他這樣的人。

» This book is **unique** because it's the only copy signed by the author.
這本書是獨一無二的，因為這是唯一作者親筆簽名的一本。

會話

A That's quite a **unique** hairstyle you've got. You look good in orange.
你的髮型很獨特，橘色很適合你。

B Very funny. The hairstylist made a mistake when she dyed it.
說起來好笑，這是髮型師在染髮時犯的錯。

usual (adj.) 平常的，通常的 ★★★★★

句型

» Jack ordered his **usual** meal. It's the one he always gets at this restaurant.
傑克點了平常吃的餐，他總是在這間餐廳點這個餐點。

» Tom and Lisa met at their **usual** time in front of the office.
湯姆和麗莎在平常時間，在辦公室前碰面。

會話

A Have you always smoked?
你一直都抽煙嗎？

B It's not a **usual** habit of mine, but every so often I have one.
這不是我平常的習慣，但偶爾會抽上一根。

usually (adv.) 通常地 

句型

» We **usually** buy our food at a supermarket.
我們通常在超市買食物。

» Peter and Alice don't **usually** go out on the weekends, unless there's a party.
彼得和愛麗絲不常在週末出去，除非有舉辦舞會。

會話

A Do you always watch TV lying down?
你總是躺著看電視嗎？

B Usually. It's more comfortable this way.
通常是，這樣比較舒服。

jealous 嫉妒的；吃醋的	34
join 參加；加入	186
joke 笑話；開玩笑	217
kilogram 公斤	217
kilometer 公里	218
kind (adj.) 仁慈的	35
kind (n.) 種類	35
kindergarten 幼稚園	77
lady 女士；淑女	36
lawyer 律師	36
lay 放置	186
lesson 課	77
let 讓	187
lie 說謊	188
lie 躺	187
lift 提起；順便搭載	188
local 當地的	159
lock (n.) 鎖	108
lock (v.) 鎖上	108
locked (adj.) 鎖上的	109
lonely 寂寞的	37
lucky (adj.) 幸運的	239
lunch 午餐	127
main (adj.) 主要的	239
male (n./ adj.) 男性；男性的；雄性的	37
manager (n.) 經理	38
mango 芒果	127
married 結婚的	38
math 數學	78
maximum 最大值	218
meaning 意義	219
meat 肉	128
menu 菜單	128
microwave 微波爐	109
mind (v.) 介意	189
minimum 最小值	219
minor (adj.) 次要的	240
mirror 鏡子	110
mix 混合	189
mop 拖地	110
mosquito 蚊子	220
multiply 乘	78
music 音樂	79
musician 音樂家	39
national (adj.) 國家的	240
necklace 項鍊	39
need 需要	190
negative (adj.) 負面的；不好的	241
neighbor 鄰居	40
nephew 姪兒；外甥	40
nervous 緊張的	41
niece 姪女；外甥女	41
noise 噪音	220
nurse 護士	42
nut 核果	129
obey 遵守；遵照	79

國家圖書館出版品預行編目資料

背單字有好方法---5大方法，快速翻轉你的英語單字力 / Howie Philips著; 張中倩譯 -- 初版. -- 新北市：布可屋文化, 2016.3
面； 公分. --（自學系列；04）
ISBN 978-986-92076-8-3（平裝附光碟片）

1.英國語言---詞彙

805.12 105003082

自學系列：04

書名 / 背單字有好方法 ---5 大方法，快速翻轉你的英語單字力
主編 / Robert Shih
著者 / Howie Philips
翻譯 / 張中倩
出版單位 / 布可屋文化
責任編輯 / 莫菲
封面設計 / Co Co House
內文排版 / Yo Yo
出版者 / 六六八企業有限公司
地址 / 新北市中和區捷運路 105 號 8F

email / bookhouse68@Gmail.com
電話／（02）2943-6268
傳真／（02）2943-6268
出版日期／ 2016 年 3 月
台幣定價／ 299 元（附 MP3）
港幣定價／ 100 元（附 MP3）

總代理／易可數位行銷股份有限公司
地址／新北市新店區寶橋路 235 巷 6 弄 3 號 5 樓
電話／（02）8911-0825
傳真／（02）8911-0801